SPRIGS OF HAWTHORN
Twelve Short Stories

Vincenzo Tedeschi
Illustrated by the author

MINERVA PRESS
LONDON
MONTREUX   LOS ANGELES   SYDNEY

SPRIGS OF HAWTHORN
Copyright © Vincenzo Tedeschi 1997

ISBN 1 86106 621 X

First published 1997 by
MINERVA PRESS
195 Knightsbridge
London SW7 1RE

Printed in Great Britain for Minerva Press

SPRIGS OF HAWTHORN

Twelve Short Stories

A Olga dedico

Tu che con gli Angeli sei,
Non esser mesta
se il pianto
agli occhi miei sovente affiora;
é solo un eco di quella gioia
che mi donasti.

*In translating from the Italian the help of my friends
Sandy Roger, William Murray and John Robertson
is acknowledged with thanks.*

Introduction

In writing these stories the author's only aim might have been to preserve memories of intensely emotional moments which left a profound impression on his early life and which otherwise might have faded, as all things, into the mist of time.

His reminiscences bring back to life a bygone world of engrossing events and colourful characters which form the fabric of these arresting and convincing stories.

The plots are woven with gripping immediacy and directness while the author himself remains discretely in the background.   His approach to people is respectful and non-judgmental; his characters have feelings, habits and problems which are both generally understandable and deeply personal.

The events take place in a remote village of Southern Italy, in the prisoner of war camps and in Scotland were the author has spent a large part of his life.   While his characters face their everyday problems in a simple and straightforward way, the incidents and events reflect general human experiences which transcend place and time.   The truths which emerge from the subtle shifts of emphasis and colour break down the barriers between fact and fiction.

Isabella Taddeo.

The Boar Hunt

When a new lot of prisoners arrived at the POW camps in Egypt or India, South Africa or Britain, the norm was to stand in wait at the gates for the chance of spotting a relative or friend from your own village or town among the newcomers, and when this happened the meeting was tense and full of emotion. "Have you seen any of my people? How are they? How long have you been away from home? Have they received my news? This is a bit of good luck, we can stay together until we go back home."

Unfortunately, it was a different matter when two villagers, Michele Santone and Rocco Zurro, met at the gate of one of these POW camps; two plain and simple chaps thrown into the tumult of war unaware of what it was all about. They only knew that when you are in the army, you must obey. While Michele was still feeling proud of a past 'triumph', if that is what it could be called, Rocco, on account of his friend's self-styled triumph and a sense of loyalty to the master of the day (meaning his Army Captain) held him culpable for the immense tragedy that befell Italy and the world; the cause of so much destruction and death.

As soon as they spotted each other, Michele raised his arms in an unashamed display of joy, running towards his old friend, but Rocco went pale with rage. "You!" he shouted, "You!" launching himself at Michele's throat while the latter tried to shield himself from the assault not able to understand why.

He could never have believed nor suspected that the origin of Rocco's strange behaviour stemmed from his own act of boldness in achieving his triumph, in disregard of all the advice and pleading for restraint which had caused Rocco's displeasure. Circumstances, finally, and the passage of time had allowed the memories in Rocco's mind to fester until the boil burst.

It all happened as a result of an unfortunate conclusion to the annual Boar Hunt at their native village a few years earlier, but, it must be said, there are quite a number of extenuating circumstances on Rocco's side. He was, in fact, the kind of person who incites some people to compassion and others to scorn and ridicule. He was what is commonly termed the village idiot. He also had an inherent quality of absorbing one particular notion at a time until he was completely obsessed.

Rocco and Michele were the only porters of the village, and were responsible for everything; wheat, wine, cereals, olive oil and any other goods that had to be carried on the backs of the men through the narrow cobbled alleys to the merchant's depot or on carts for the railway station. Rocco was as strong as a mule. Rough-looking, short and square like a cement block, pimply and quite often unshaven, he was not a pretty sight. His long arms hung down from his broad shoulders to below the hips, terminating in small, fat hands, and the general impression of strength prevented anyone from fooling with him.

Michele, on the other hand, although strong enough to tackle the kind of job he was doing, did not look strong. He had small features and an intelligent face which looked rather cunning. This was the reason why he had managed to inflict his commands upon Rocco, saving the lighter loads and less frequent journeys for himself.

Before the war they had been inseparable and looked as if the one could not do without the other. Rocco did most of the work and

Michele collected the money and paid him any amount without being questioned.

However, this changed dramatically when, against all advice, warnings and threats from his friend, Rocco took a wife.

Michele felt as though the earth had suddenly opened up under his feet and, while finally accepting the fait accompli, he tried hard to maintain his hold on Rocco. But Concetta, Rocco's bride, had her own ideas. She was a little woman, quite round and plain, with a face made mannish by a slight hint of a moustache, a short wide nose and generally adverse features, which she amply compensated for with a vivacious personality. Already in her early thirties and dreading a long spinsterhood, she set her eyes on Rocco finding, needless to say, soft and fertile ground.

From there on Rocco would, in effect, have to content himself with two bosses, even though there was no doubt who would gain the upper hand. But there was no time for one or the other to dominate completely, even though Concetta was well on her way to dominating both of them. After only two months of marriage, both men were recalled to the army; Michele into a labourer's unit of the Engineers Brigade and Rocco to his old Infantry Regiment at Sulmona, where Captain Bergoni was so pleased to see him that he was almost on the verge of kissing him. Having fished Rocco instantly from the group of recalled men still in their civilian clothes, the captain took him to the kitchen for a good meal, then to the uniform store and finally to his room where, right away, he was put to work polishing his boots. It is not easy to see what else this strong chap could have done in the army, or by what standards he had enlisted in the first place, except for his physique and an apparently servile inclination.

With their army unit, Rocco and his captain were both taken prisoners in a battle with an Australian unit on the stony embankment of Derma. Transported to a POW camp in South Africa, they remained as before, a captain and his orderly; the captain and half a dozen officers in one tent and their orderlies in another.

The idleness and boredom induced the officers to indulge in long discussions on the conduct of the war and the orderlies were compelled to listen to them, not altogether passively.

To blame Il Duce could have proven to be a dangerous indiscretion. Therefore, the blame for all those military disasters would inevitably fall upon the Minister of War, who had not made proper preparations and plans. Just as a slow drop of water can wear away a stone, the accusations against this Minister were building in Rocco's head day after day, until he became so obsessed and full of hate for him, that if the man had appeared there and then, he would have strangled him. Even worse, his hatred was building towards his old friend Michele whom, during the Boar Hunt some years earlier, against the will of Concetta, his wife, arrogantly sprinted into the thick undergrowth of the forest to achieve glory – at least that's what he said it was – and thereby created a tragedy so great that even his captain could have become a victim, never mind so many others in the world.

As we said, the story of this arrogance and boasting goes back to the Boar Hunt beat in the forest in their native village.

The Boar Hunt, reserved for the village gentry, was in effect a social occasion and a good excuse for a fine picnic in the open air. Unfortunately, there was only a sprinkling of boars left, while the scrubby undergrowth of the ancient oak trees was so thick as to make sheltering easy for the few animals still surviving. Except for a few beaten tracks, the forest was quite impenetrable. Another element in favour of boars was the tales of people having been slaughtered or maimed by ferocious animals with tusks as long as a blood-letting knife.

This particular beat happened only a few weeks after Rocco's wedding. As usual, the village was feverishly preparing for it. The village policeman, a very fat, short man with a nose like a large red pepper, was busy recruiting the beaters, those who make loud noises in order to direct the prey towards the guns, and booking the horses and mules, while a committee of councillors and gentry was preparing the list of guests and participants.

That year, though, things turned out differently from any other year when all went as smoothly as oil on water, all because news came that a big fascist Party Chief would be coming for the Hunt. This sent the village into a sort of frenzy.

In the first instance, in order not to disappoint the high-ranking illustrious guest, the meagre game had to be protected from those who had made a habit of plundering it, (to judge from the amount of black boar sausage freely available), and it was also necessary to alter or amend the list of participants.

To defend the forest, or the boars, the militia were given strict orders to concentrate attention mainly and solely on this task, with some help from the provincial command, which sent three extra men. This way the professional timber and log-sellers were given a free hand in the other part of the forest, to the benefit of the villagers who bought firewood at reasonable prices.

Redrawing the guest list was no easy matter. At a noisy meeting of the committee it was decided to eliminate a few gentlemen with suspicious political ideas to make room for at least four high officials who would accompany the high-ranking personality.

Someone started a rumour that the personality was Il Duce himself. Most people did not believe this though. "Il Duce?... he always goes hunting in Maremma."

"Yes!" someone else added in a whisper, and "through the good offices of the municipal tax collectors!"...

But the rumours that it was indeed Il Duce were slowly gaining strength and credibility. "Just imagine!... Il Duce at Grottole!... the neighbouring villages would die of envy!" Especially Miglionico, which had a not-so-glorious controversial memory of Il Duce in the past. A year earlier, on occasion of the Grand Army manoeuvres in the Irpinian Mountains, Il Duce decided to detour to the south to see how the indigenous people there lived. Starting from Foggia, having bypassed the Murgia Country in Apulia, he strayed into Basilicata which was well off the beaten track. On the main road between Matera and Potenza, standing erect on a touring car he accepted the applause and greetings of the poor villagers; sometimes, on walkabout, he would kiss a baby or two but, when he reached Miglionico, where the preparations to receive him had been carried out with scrupulous attention to detail, even anticipating a speech from the flag-draped podium, the motorcade sped past the large crowd lining both sides of the road, leaving a huge cloud of dust and making it quite impossible to identify the figure of Il Duce among all those ornamented caps.

Perhaps the people of Miglionico would have tolerated the impoliteness but Il Duce, evidently subject to some irresistible impulse, was unable to avoid adding insult to injury when, about half a mile beyond the village near the Cemetery, the motorcade suddenly stopped. Il Duce jumped out of the car, greatly alarming the Generals and officers with him, and quickly ran behind a bush to answer an urgent call of nature.

The Grottolese have a great respect for the Miglionico people, but they say they are a bit vain and take things a bit too much to heart. Indeed, among the many faithful who felt offended – some even burning their black shirts – there were those who at the site of the "ugly" act proposed to build a monument.

One can imagine the bile of the Miglionico people if Il Duce had indeed come to Grottole for the Boar Hunt.

However, a few days before the Hunt, unfortunately, it was learnt with a sense of disappointment that the famous personality was not to be Il Duce, but his Minister of War who would arrive the day before the Hunt.

The part-time Fascist Militia, the M.V.S.N., began patrolling the road up to the Cantoniera, within the village boundary, their rifles intended for show because there was no ammunition.

The day on which the War Minister was due to arrive, the whole village converged on the little square and along the main street. The school children, dressed in their Fascist uniforms by their teachers, were placed in the front row of the crowd while a young boy bugler, dressed in his black shirt, sounded "stand to attention" as soon as he spotted the line of cars.

One after the other the automobiles stopped in front of the Town Hall where the local dignitaries were waiting with gooeyd anxiety.

Under the amazed eyes of the crowd, the car doors opened. First to alight was a very robust man in Fascist uniform who pushed aside some of the local Party officers trying to be the first to greet the Minister and set his hawk-like eyes all around, keeping his hand firmly on a large pistol by his side. Then came a number of Fascist officers and finally the Minister himself. Surrounded as he was by so many of his own men and local dignitaries, the only sign that he was alighting was his small hand held high in a Roman salute. In fact, His Excellency was a skeletal individual no taller than one metre sixty. The large gilt braided visor hid a bony face with deep-set black eyes under a wide forehead, over a thin pointed chin.

Before anyone could shout: "Hurrah... Hurrah... he was led into the atrium of the Town Hall. The people in the crowd waited some five to ten minutes in case there was to be a speech from the balcony, and soon they dispersed through the village streets.

After the refreshments, the personalities were boarded with local dignitaries until the following morning when the Hunt would start.

During the night a sprinkling of snow had given the early morning a kind of wintry look but the crystal clear sky heralded a beautiful day to come. In the little square the mules, horses and donkeys were being assembled for the hunters and services, such as the transportation of groceries, wine, chairs and crockery, while the beaters with a dozen dogs of all kinds and sizes were waiting, segregated, in the neighbourhood of the post office. The robust fellow in black shirt and leather bandoleer full of ammunition, who could have been the Minister's bodyguard, was asking about the programme for the day and when he was told the Minister had been given a position devoid of any danger, he improvised a speech on the spot for the benefit of the local dignitaries. He said, "The Duce would be furious," and he added, "this kind of treatment belongs to the old decadent and reactionary bourgeoisie; by the example we get from him, all of us must face dangers with the same heroic spirit of the Fascist Revolution. In our party there is no room for cowardice."

After this speech His Excellency was given the inner position at the thickest part of the forest where a number of boars' paths crossed in all directions; the most prolific hunting position, but also the most dangerous.

His Excellency arrived in the square accompanied by a beautiful collie he called Littorio. The dog became the object of thoughtful attention.

Littorio looked cross; maybe he declared it beneath his dignity to mix with the scruffy pack of dogs assembled for the hunt. He was put in the safe hands of the local policeman. When parting with it the Minister looked distinctly nervous. He gave the policeman some instructions on how to deal with the dog, especially since it belonged to his wife. He asked the man if he was married so he would understand what he meant. The Minister did not like to part with it, but he could not put it on a donkey, could he?

The Minister's bodyguard kept close to him, always ready to reach for his gun, while Don Luca, the old retired elementary schoolteacher, who was always suspected of being a liberal, was pointing his long marine telescope at him, rather than the Minister, and any time his head came into focus, he bent his index finger as if pulling a trigger.

He hated the Blackshirts, but fortunately the local authorities had a great respect for him.

At a short distance from the square they were loading the requirements for the picnic. Who else was suitably able to attend to this business than the two porters, Rocco and Michele. The two men were ably assisted by Rocco's wife, or rather, the two of them were assisting her, since she had by now established a certain control over both men, a fact which greatly annoyed Michele as he now began to resent and fear her.

Once everyone was mounted on horseback, the caravan set off from the forest accompanied by the deafening noise of steel-shod hooves on the cobbles and followed closely by the policeman with His Excellency's dog on a leash. They were followed some distance away by the mules transporting the provisions for the picnic. Concetta was comfortably ensconced on one of the mules and the two friends followed behind on foot.

On arriving at the forest which covered a conical hill half way down the valley, they set up their base camp in a clearing, while the beaters and hunters left to take up their assigned positions. The local policeman led the Minister and his bodyguard, with the dog, to the assigned positions and, on leaving, he told them he would return to take them to the picnic area at one o'clock.

The forest began to resound with the barking of dogs and the beating of sticks on trees. The birds fluttered frightened from tree to tree and now and then a rustling through the bushes made it seem as though a boar were about to appear.

The Minister threw up his double-barrelled shotgun to shoot on several occasions in vain, but, suddenly, there was more heavy rustling and a terrified young boar burst out of the bushes. His Excellency shouldered his gun to shoot once again, but at the same moment Littorio, the dog, pulled strongly on the leash and burst free to dash off, barking furiously, in pursuit of the animal.

The Minister let the gun fall from his shaking fingers, rushed out of his safe position and started running after his dog, yelling: "Littorio!... Littorio!... Come back." The dog, however, simply would not listen, so intent was he in chasing after the boar. In no time he had disappeared into the thick undergrowth with the Minister and his bodyguard in hot pursuit, desperately shouting "Littorio!... Littorio!... "

Pushing hard through the thick bushes they became quite exhausted and were soon dripping with sweat. Still shouting the dog's name, they tried to retrace their steps to their starting point. The dogs continued to bark in all directions but the footpaths had disappeared and the bush was becoming increasingly thicker and quite impenetrable.

Having reached the previously agreed position and failed to find the Minister, the local policeman ran off to raise the alarm.

Once he had gathered around him everyone who was there, the Master of the Hunt tried to organise a search. He was counting greatly on the co-operation of the beaters, so he promised a reward of fifty lire to anyone who found a trace of the Minister.

At the end of the appeal Concetta, seeing the flush of avarice on her husband's face, caught him by the arm and took him behind a bush.

"Hide in there, quick!" she ordered.

"What?... why?... " poor Rocco protested.

"I said hide!" she repeated, "or else I'll leave you here and go home."

In came Michele, with a large stick in his hand, ready to move off: "Come on!... What are you waiting for?... Get yourself a stick and come with me."

"You too," shouted Concetta. "Hide yourself; don't be stupid. Don't you know that there are huge boars in there, with tusks capable of ripping half your leg off?" But Michele did not listen.

"Come on, or I'll go myself," he shouted at his friend.

"You stupid ass! Go on! Go in there if you like, but you'll just get yourself killed!"

Concetta was not to be moved. She pushed her husband into the large bush. Confused and intimidated, the poor chap had to watch as Michele disappeared.

The efforts to trace the Minister and his bodyguard had been going on for an hour or two, with a dozen or so of the local party bigwigs all trying to direct operations. Suddenly Michele Zuffo emerged triumphantly from the bushes, his shirt and trousers in tatters and with scratches all over his body, yelling: "I've found him!... I ... me... I found him!"

Soon afterwards, His Excellency and the bodyguard emerged from the bushes. They were hardly recognisable, thoroughly humiliated and exhausted, and they looked like a couple of beggars.

In the meantime, Michele was passing from person to person in the crowd, shouting: "It was me; yes, I'm the one who saved him!" Turning to his friend, he gave him the finger. From that moment on the friendship took a decisive turn for the worse, or, truth to tell, it ended there and then.

So, too, ended that year's Boar hunt. Not a shot was fired nor a boar killed.

When the two saw each other again at the POW camp, it was the very day on which Rocco had taken one of those notions which, in his case, obliterated all other thoughts and had become an obsession. Consequently, in that state of mind, there is nothing more compelling towards violent actions than the opportunity to carry them out shortly after pondering the actions; before the rage, the will and the nerves have a chance to cool off.

That was the very day the officers had been having a long and lively argument on the causes and the conduct of the war, and especially the Italian defeats, while their orderlies served tea and listened to the arguments with feigned disinterest.

Weaponry was inadequate; the logistic services were inefficient; the Air Force was only equipped with old and useless planes; the Navy was too precious to risk on the high seas and the soldiers had little or no training. None of this was Mussolini's fault, of course. The blame lay with party officials, the generals and ministers who all kept him in the dark about everything. Actually, the blame lay mostly with the Minister of War who was a relative of Il Duce or a friend of a friend of the King, who carried little weight and even less authority in the Ministry.

These discussions continued in the orderlies' tent with even greater emphasis, so much so, they almost ended in a fight. Each orderly praised his own officer's point of view:

"What about the tanks, what state were, or rather are they in? A pea-shooter could have destroyed them!"

"And the Artillery?... the guns are all First World War vintage, at least that's what my Lieutenant says."

"And the petrol?... Just go to the depot and what do they tell you? 'There's none today; there may be some tomorrow'... and what if we are attacked? We can't move; some bloody war."

"And what did the Minister of War do? He slept, that's what. 'And for us soldiers, to suffer and die'."

Rocco Santone was listening to all this, absorbing and accumulating a rage which seemed to make his very blood boil. Finally, with a grunt which seemed to emanate from the mouth of a wolf, leaving everyone terrified, he started shouting:

"Bastard!... Pig!... I'll kill him!"

All eyes turned to look at him with apprehension.

"Who?... who are you talking about?"

"Michele... Michele... that swine!... I'll kill him!"

"What are you saying... who is this Michele... why?... "

"He's the one! It was him that saved that stinking Minister!... When I get back to the village, I'll kill him!"

The poor chap had, no doubt, been seized by an attack of schizophrenia. With his bloodshot eyes and foaming mouth, he was a sight fit to terrify. At that moment someone announced that a convoy of new POWs was arriving. The orderlies all began running towards the main gate, followed by Rocco who looked more as though he were chasing the enemy than running to get to the gate.

When he saw Michele, the man he held responsible for saving the life of the Minister of War, among the first arrivals he went wild with rage. He threw himself at Michele's throat, his hands outstretched like a vice and would doubtless have killed him, had not a dozen people pulled him off the unfortunate chap who, between bouts of coughing and the effort of regaining his breath, shouted:

"He is crazy. He is out of his mind."

A Kiss To Sylvia

The large liner which had transported us from South Africa put down anchor five hundred yards, or so it looked, off the coast at Greenock, on the Clyde. Both banks of the wide estuary looked so peaceful! It was springtime and the air was filled with scents of pine and heather, and in the distance some avenues made a great show of apple or cherry blossom. We landed by a transfer to pontoons and directly boarded a waiting train which left quickly for our destination. We knew later the name of the little town down the green valley; it was called Denny.

We had to build our own tents and as soon as we got settled the contractors arrived and we were put to digging foundation trenches and setting the roads level. The huts which were prefabricated went up quickly and in no time the POW camp was ready.

With my good friend Donnarumma we established the Administration Office adjacent the Command Hut, supervised by Accounts Officer Lt. Wilkinson and Private Franklin, who was a member the church of Christ Scientist of Massachusetts and at every spare moments stuck his head into the Christian Science Monitor.

Most POWs were taken to work on farms, some others to a paper mill. As soon as we were completely settled we thought about some sort of recreational activity. Someone organised a football team which was soon to challenge the village team, not always without success. Donnarumma and I got permission and assistance from the Camp Commandant to build a stage in the recreation hut and soon managed to organise some shows. These were a mixture of sing-song and comedy. A number of Italian expatriates living in the surrounding area were allowed into the camp to watch the shows: you could see their emotions – at times they would burst into tears. They were mostly old people who had left their little villages, some fifty or sixty years ago, peasants and labourers with no education, only a will to work. While doing this they had had to endure provocation and insults for many years before their perseverance succeeded in gaining them respect and admiration. It was at one of these shows that I met Mrs Profetti.

She lived in a village about five miles from the camp, and as I was given a bicycle in order to visit the POWs billeted on farm to arrange for their banking operations (five shillings per week), I had no difficulty in getting to her home. There I found that I was not alone: there were another four or five chaps there who lived on the nearby farms. Our welcome was so wholehearted that we soon made a habit, every other evening, of being there.

Mrs Profetti was a woman of about fifty years of age. She had been a widow for more than ten years and respecting Italian customs, always dressed in black. There was, however, nothing to suggest that she still felt grief at her long bereavement: she was always glad to see us welcoming us with open arms and occasionally with a kiss.

She had certainly never been what could be called beautiful and the many wrinkles on her olive coloured face revealed a past of loneliness, sorrow and sacrifice in bringing up the two youngsters who on their father's death could here been no more than seven and ten years of age.

Sylvia, her daughter, was now seventeen and a girl of great vivacity. She never seemed to walk, she ran all the time. She was inclined to a little stoutness and while running, due to the excess weight she carried, her chest swayed quite innocently as she moved.

Her chestnut hair fell in plaits over her neck and plump shoulders. Her eyes were green and bright; she flashed them restlessly, and they sparkled like diamonds and they seemed to be always searching, enquiring. Her full lips ended in two dimples which formed a sort of constant smile.

She could have been beautiful were it not for a slightly large Tuscan nose which seemed to be put there to spite her.

We had established a completely familial relationship with the Profettis, both mother and daughter, and since the mother regarded us as sons, as she herself kept repeating, it was impossible to treat the girl other than a sister. Deep down, though, Mrs Profetti nursed aspiration and she hoped in a future for her daughter with one of us, just like in a romantic novel, mostly because she would not have wished her to marry a Protestant as probabilities would suggest.

When she learned, some months later, that I was going out with an Italian girl from Glasgow, some twenty-five miles from the concentration camp, she was disappointed, and stood in shock for a few seconds. For the first time I noticed on her face what must have been an enduring sadness. She raised her chin and slightly square jaw as though to clench her teeth, before a visibly forced smile appeared on her face and she regained her composure.

"Good!" she said, "She is a fine-looking girl. I know her." And we never spoke of it again.

She knew from my sudden blush that I had fallen in love and, hiding her obvious disappointment, she continued to treat me just like the others. For my part, I felt sorrow and guilt, and from that day on I began really to like her. She had, without doubt, become my second mother.

And Sylvia said, "You have really fallen for her, have you?"

I did not reply.

Afterwards, I had the impression that Sylvia, not having had an answer, was trying to hook me with extraordinary charm. This depressed me because I understood that my efforts at remaining indifferent and pretending not to notice made her angry.

In a few weeks time, however, things returned to normal and since, due to the distance, I saw my girl only on Sundays when she came to the camp with her mother or to visit her cousin in the country, our evenings spent with the Profettis were a delight.

We had hardly reached their house when they served us fried fish, hot and crisp, from the fish and chip shop on the ground floor; then there was conversation, reminiscences and the records, all scratched and faulty, of Italian songs. Sometimes we danced, especially when one or two Italian girls from the neighbourhood happened to come round "on the off chance". I was happy to have rediscovered family life, respect and unselfish affection for these two women.

Mrs Profetti had again become her good-natured self and continued to seem cheerful, with that fun-loving cheerfulness which is a special feature of the Tuscan character. Everything went well until she came out with the name Alberto. "Alberto, my poor little lad!... Dear Alberto!... My baby..."

This Alberto was Mrs Profetti's eldest son and we couldn't stand him from the first time she spoke his name. Where was Alberto?... First in North Africa with the British forces, then in Italy, at Caserta to be exact.

On Armistice Day, she called out joyfully to us as we arrived at the house one after the other: "Alberto!... He's landed in Italy. Mussolini has fallen and now there's that Marshal – What's his name?"

"Badoglio," replied Sylvia.

Alberto Profetti was a corporal in the British army and, although we knew the circumstances, the idea that a son of Italians should be our enemy left us bewildered.

"Poor boy. Born here, a British subject," she moaned – rightly – "he couldn't refuse. They'd have thrown him in jail and his whole life would have been ruined."

Her reasons were valid, yet we couldn't forgive him. In our hearts he was our enemy.

But Mrs Profetti had no notion of our anger and every now and then, as though she did it on purpose, up would bring that hated name. "Alberto has been a student, you know? He's very intelligent and when he's demobbed, he'll continue his studies to be a lawyer, not like us ignoramuses. He'll set himself up in his own professional office with a great big desk and books all round the walls, you'll see! Not like us old ones who've toiled and sweated in this wretched fish and chip shop. Nearly all the children of Italians are studying now, and in ten years time not one will be running a fish and chip shop: they'll all be lawyers, engineers, teachers or even MPs."

We liked to hear this reasoning; perhaps we could forgive him in that far-off future but, for the moment, not likely. Deep down, our resentment and hate persisted despite all our efforts at goodwill.

One evening after supper – consisting of the usual bag of fish and chips – they wanted to show us the album full of photographs of Alberto: "This is him at six years old... Here he is at seven with his dad (God rest his soul); here he is at school with his pals, he was twelve then. Here we are, this one was taken just before he went into the army. And this one, just look how handsome he is in his regimental uniform. The Gordon Highlanders."

May God forgive us, but it only made things worse.

We would have preferred to forget Alberto, but the price of putting up with him was insignificant compared with the many kindnesses the two women showed us. They had, in all sincerity, conquered our hearts which were desperate for sympathy and comfort after so many years of torment and isolation.

Thus we continued to put up with him for a long time, and when at last Germany capitulated, we began to feel some sympathy for him, with a little reservation. After all, poor chap, what else could he do?... Right was on his side, but making it understood to your deepest instincts was another matter entirely.

*

The end of hostilities put us all in a fever of anxiety to return home. Letters from Italy, and correspondence in general which during the war years had been practically non-existent, was resumed, causing joy for many and problems for others: unfaithful wives, sisters fallen into disgrace, brothers killed and all the other calamities and horrors of defeat. Some had lost their whole families, others their houses and all their possessions, and amid all the cheerfulness there often emerged weeping and despair. Two of the prisoners ended up in the Mental Hospital and the memory of one of them, the camp barber, makes me shiver yet. They took him away submissive as a sheep, his glassy eyes staring into nothing and murmuring four words over and over, as though in a litany: "Hello... Pasqua... it's me. Hello... Pasqua... it's me.

Many more months passed before repatriation began. First the wounded, then in order of age the oldest till finally I, being one of the younger, was left as the Profettis' only visitor.

Mrs Profetti had waited till the last minute to tell me something and ask me a favour. Had I known how it would end and despite the respect, affection and gratitude I owed her, I would have refused the favour she asked of me without regret, that is if my conscience would have allowed it.

But I agreed, naively, to do it – a matter of taking a parcel to Alberto in Caserta. Unblinking, I said impulsively, "Why, certainly!" I was about to add, "It'll be a pleasure to meet Alberto," but the unrelenting antipathy I nursed towards him assailed me secretly, and I refrained.

"A little parcel for Alberto; you must do me this favour."

"Favour?... Not a bit of it – it's s an obligation, a duty. Why certainly."

"It won't be too much trouble? It's not out of your way?"

"No trouble at all," I replied. "I'd take it, even were it to the North Pole instead of Caserta!" How could anyone possibly refuse Mrs Profetti this one favour which meant so much to her?

"You are the one I can trust; you know you've been my favourite because you're like a son to me, just like my Alberto: shy, gentle, kind-hearted."

"No, no, good heavens, please!" I murmured in embarrassment.

"There you go, you're blushing, just like my own boy. My Alberto will be so pleased to meet you! I've written and told him so much about you. I've told him you are like a son to me. For that matter, I think I've been like a mother to the rest of you as well."

"Of course you have," I assured her. "We are all extremely grateful to you."

She said she would give me the parcel the following Sunday, a few days before my transfer to the transit camp prior to repatriation.

Considering the time we would spend in the transit camp, then the journey and so on, the parcel would have got there quicker by post, but I forbore to mention it.

At that moment, I heard the characteristic click-clack of women's shoes on the stone stairs outside the house and into the room burst Sylvia, all breathless and smiling as ever, and hugged me effusively.

"You're going away?... You're going to find my little brother, or rather, my big brother?"

"Of course I am," I replied. She gave me a long look, not knowing what else to say, and I noticed in her shining eyes a certain sadness.

The time of departure was rapidly approaching.

"How many days now? – Ten? – And your fiancée? Will you see her again?"

"Sure," I replied. "She'll come with her mother to the town near the transit camp and they'll stay till the day of final departure."

When Mrs Profetti went out to the kitchen, Sylvia stayed behind, giving me an inquiring look, then she whispered: "But why didn't you fall for me?"

Flustered and confused, I blushed with shame. At first I didn't know what to say. Then I started mumbling: "Well... Er..." At last, in a firm tone, as though inspired, I said, "Perhaps it was because you didn't fall for me." Her eyes lit up in sudden realisation. "Ah, yes," she said, slightly embarrassed, adding in English, "We didn't click," and she gave a sad smile.

That was the last time I saw Sylvia. The following Sunday when I went to collect the parcel, she was not in, having gone out with some girl-friends. Her mother made her apologies, then gave me my final instructions.

"Please give Alberto my love. Tell him we are lonely and sad. No, tell him that we are well and that we are waiting for him."

Then she kissed me, not as effusively as usual, and stood watching me from the top of the stairs – with tears in her eyes, I think – till I disappeared on my bicycle.

"Goodbye," I said, waving with one hand as I rounded the bend on the road.

The spring sun as it set, imparted a red glow to the low clouds on the age-old, pine-clad horizon, over the verdant sweep of the Scottish hills, and there came suddenly into my mind these verses from Dante:

"... era già l'ora che volge al desio i naviganti e intenerisce il cuore,
lo dì che han detto ai dolci amici, addio!"

(The hour it was when sailors' yearning hearts grow tender,
The day on which they bade sweet friends goodbye)

Before embarkation we spent about ten days in the transit camp at Ayr, on the coast of the county or shire of that name. There we were supplied with new uniforms, without the hated yellow patch sewn on our back which identified us as Italian POWs. The Germans had a red one. Our compound was always open and we could go out at any time up till 9 p.m. – not that there was the slightest danger of anyone escaping on the very eve of repatriation. Along with my girlfriend and her mother, who never let her out of her sight, we spent a truly peaceful and intensely enjoyable time. My girl's mother was a lady of the old school, full of moral principles and still tied to the customs of the little town in Tuscany where she had lived until the day of her wedding to her old sweetheart, already established in Scotland. I had won her heart before conquering her daughter's. She seemed to like me from the very first day and, being uncommonly perceptive, at once understood our feelings. One day, while sitting on the beach some distance away from the two of us, she put down the knitting which seemed to be her constant occupation and gave us a long, close look: I noticed that she was crying. When we got up, her eyes were still moist.

"What's wrong?" I asked naively.

"Nothing... Nothing," she replied, slightly offended. Later, when my girl moved away to speak to a friend and she saw I was worried, she was once more overcome with emotion. Taking her hand I again asked: "Why, what's the matter?"

"Nothing... Nothing," and she apologised. At length, feeling that she owed me an explanation, she continued in a low voice, sobbing convulsively: "You two," she said, "I think you are made for each other," – and she could never have uttered a truer word. She loved her only daughter with an intensity which was almost possessive, if not completely so.

These days were quick in passing, divided for me between the blissfulness of the situation and an ever lively apprehension at returning home after seven years of absence.

"I'll be back," I said when we finally embarked at the port of Glasgow, and after emotional goodbyes I waved more greetings to them from the rail of the ship, while the two white handkerchiefs among the crowd gradually disappeared into the distance.

The ship sailed down the wide delta of the River Clyde, between the many greetings and good wishes coming from the banks and the small ferry steamers. Gradually the shores widened out, houses and villages became less and less distinct, as a light mist lingered over the valleys. These were full of pines, while the treeless mountains wore a festive look with their coloured heather – patches of white, pink and innumerable shades of violet. Once the Isle of Arran was behind us we were in the open sea, that grey northern sea – more grey verging on black – as the twilight shadows fell.

During the voyage I was worried about Mrs Profetti's parcel, fearing it might be lost or stolen and I did not leave the ship's hold for a whole day. Then, having become friendly with a British sailor, I asked him to keep it for me till we disembarked, which he kindly agreed to do.

On the fourth day we were in the Mediterranean and, three days later, in the Bay of Naples.

The ship took on the appearance of a human swarm: the bows, decks, lifeboats and every vantage point thronged with tense and silent men. The city drew nearer as in a dream, with its great buildings coloured terracotta, pink and lemon. Vesuvius, with its plume of white smoke, little houses dotting its terraced sides, and radiant Posillipo's smiling headland. Ah, that sea so blue, those enchanted islands in the bay! Ischia, Capri, a Siren's song seemed to be heard on every hand! Not a single one of us but wept for joy.

When we got into the harbour, however, we were overwhelmed as by a jet of icy water at the sight of the havoc and destruction, the confusion of wrecked cranes and piled-up rubble where busy warehouses and offices had once stood.

On a background of grey sea made filthy by all kinds of wreckage lay numerous ships, their sides gashed by bombs, their innards spilling out from where death surely reigned. Our joy was transmuted to silence and anguish.

We disembarked like sheep from a railway truck, one after the other, between a column of armed Italian soldiers, through an improvised office where we had to give details of the unit we belonged to, our military district and our place of residence. In another small room a captain gave us each twenty thousand lire and told us we could return to our homes, advising us to return to our military district in a fortnight for final discharge.

Thus, from a well-guarded courtyard, we were thrown onto the streets of Naples, starved and lost, each of us left to his own fate.

Nothing, however, could dim the anxious joy of homecoming, and we made straight for the railway station.

The tramcars being packed and infrequent, nearly all of us decided to walk, a slow and lugubrious procession along pavements crowded with street-urchins, prostitutes and soldiers of every race and colour: Americans, British, Australians, Indians and Blacks, while military convoys and police jeeps darted about in all directions.

This was the reality of defeat and each one of these soldiers seemed more of an enemy than when we were at the front. We shared the feeling of the peasant who, on returning from the fair, finds gangsters have beaten up his mother and, as she lay on her back, were dancing on her stomach. But, helpless and humiliated, we continued on our way to the hoped-for peace of our homes.

At the station each of us sought information on trains for his own village. "The trains," said an official, "leave when they can. For Potenza and Taranto there is one tomorrow night from platform 12.

Eagerly I went in search of platform twelve and I came across a long line of people: some sitting on bags and cases, others on foot and yet more stretched out on the ground asleep: men, women and shabbily dressed children, boredom and weariness visible on their emaciated faces.

"This train," I asked, "where is it going?"

"It's the Taranto train," came the answer.

"Is there one today as well?"

"No. Tomorrow night."

I had intended to spend the night in a hotel, but after buying a couple of sandwiches and a bottle of wine, I took my place at the tail-end of the queue which was gradually getting longer till it extended outside the station.

After an exhausting wait of twenty-six hours the Taranto train came in: one ancient engine and five rickety carriages.

To begin with the passengers went aboard in orderly fashion; then they started jostling, shouting and scuffling. I managed to find a seat on a wooden bench while the carriage became crammed with people, some even occupying the spaces reserved for luggage.

A few hours later the train set off, puffing and panting, and after nine hours and a thousand stops in the darkness of night arrived at Grottole station. It was ten o'clock on the morning of Easter Sunday, 1946.

Here I was at last, after seven years, back among my own folk, and ten days later I could still hardly believe it. I felt like the

Australian boomerang which, hurled willy-nilly into the air, by some aerodynamic mystery returns safely to its point of departure in the hands of the thrower. I was overjoyed at having come back unscathed from so many accidents and lucky escapes from danger, machine-gun bullets from planes spattering all around on the sand like stones on a pond, my tank on fire after being hit; followed by capture, the long desert march from Agedabia to Benghazi, hungry and thirsty beneath the merciless sun and the thousand other incredible dangers I had escaped from. For this I felt grateful to the divine hand that had caused them to come so close without touching me. I had gone away as a boy of seventeen and now came back a man moulded by bitter experience, wiser, more mature. But not wise enough to give up the idea of taking to Alberto at Caserta the parcel from his mother. At home they begged me: "Send it by post, don't go. Travelling is so difficult in these harsh times."

Needless to say, I didn't listen. What would Mrs Profetti think? It was very important to me not to seem ungrateful and neglectful. I had made a promise and I would keep it. Besides, I didn't want to lose credit in Mrs Profetti's eyes; it would have been such an undeserved disappointment to her! So, some ten days after my arrival home I set off – helped by a little cash from my parents – for the railway station. I felt as if I had already forgiven Alberto for being in the enemy camp. After all, we had almost (as people say) a mother in common.

I still had the knapsack they had given us in Britain and I thought it would be less noticeable than a small suitcase. Into it I packed Alberto's parcel, a shirt, some underpants, handkerchiefs and socks, my shaving things and, tied up in a napkin, bread, sausage, cheese and a flask of wine – a wooden one, of the type widely used by country folk in southern Italy.

The train was about forty minutes late. I started to wander about the station and looked up at the little town, its jagged outline faintly silhouetted by a few dim lights against the glimmering whiteness of dawn behind the hill.

It was already daylight when the train at last drew into the station and the sun emerged, huge and brilliant, like a crucible of liquid gold, over the clayey slope between Grottole and Miglionico. It was the same train I had travelled in from Naples; in fact it was the only one on this line, going north to south one day and south to north the next.

To my astonishment the train wasn't overcrowded, maybe because it was a Monday or maybe there were more convenient trains running from Taranto to Bari, Rome and the North. Anyway, the compartment in which I took a seat contained only one other passenger. He was stretched out on one of the long wooden makeshift benches, his head covered with a sheet of newspaper and resting on a kind of soldier's knapsack. On the corridor side of the seat opposite were two large suitcases, one on top of the other. I would have left him in peace had I not been attracted by the unoccupied window seat, those in the other compartments being taken. On seeing me he removed the paper from his face and sat up in surprise and annoyance. I took my seat, nodding a greeting, but he went on staring at me without batting an eye. I turned away pretending to arrange my bag, and shortly afterwards I put it up on the luggage-rack, just in order to make a move unconcernedly; but when I resumed my seat I met once more his sullen eyes staring at me. Amazed at this behaviour and realising the kind of person I was confronting, I stared hard back at him for a long while until he gave in, turned his head away and lay down as before, pretending to sleep.

Clearly my fellow passenger must be some kind of crook. He had four or five days' growth of beard, just merging with sideburns from thick, dirty hair which came down over his forehead almost to the eyebrows. His sharp eyes, of an intense light-blue, were like those of a bird of prey. The fingers of his pale, thin hands were extra long. Though he was decently enough dressed and wearing military ribbons, his battered shoes hadn't seen a vestige of polish since they were new.

Although he kept restlessly turning and moving from side to side, he gave me no trouble as far as Potenza. So, I was able to look at and reflect on the countryside, whose green was gashed by landslips in the little fields that stood on the margin of fearsome precipices; the donkeys and mules clambering up steep pathways.

Were my eyes changed from the time I was a boy and saw things in a different light? Those poor folk behind their mules, the tiny strips of unproductive soil, rocky and collapsing – how they distressed me.

Slowly, slowly, puffing and with shrill, angry whistles, the train reached the approaches to Potenza. We had just passed Vaglio Lucano station, on the final steep assent to the town's main station, when a very thin young man, his shirt hanging outside his long, flared trousers – I had seen him dozens of times walking up and down the corridor – burst into the compartment. Bowing, and apologising in his Neapolitan dialect, he started beseeching me effusively, almost penitentially:

"Oh, please, Your Honour, respected sir... In Heaven's name: I must open the window. I do beg your pardon, Sir, for the inconvenience, but I have to get rid of these suitcases. What a terrible job... But, hunger! People are dying of hunger, and they do so need something to eat."

My odd-looking fellow passenger got up and went out into the corridor. I got up also and took a seat on the opposite side near the door.

When the carriage door was fully opened we were blinded by dense black smoke as the train toiled upwards at not more than six miles an hour. The young man seized the heavy suitcases and dropped them out, one at a time, at predetermined points where no doubt somebody was waiting. So the cases did not belong to my odd companion, and evidently contained goods intended for the black market.

At Potenza a large crowd awaiting us on the platform stormed into the carriages. My companion took the seat opposite me near the door, and half a dozen country people with bundles and parcels occupied the empty places. I felt safer now, and during the descent to Salerno, what with the stifling heat, weariness, the effects of the blinding smoke and spent sparks, plus the fact that I was dripping with sweat and weakened by constant efforts to stay alert, I carelessly sank into a deep sleep.

I must have slept more than two hours, for when I awoke we weren't far from Eboli. I was just about to light a cigarette when I remembered I was hungry. I got up to take down my knapsack but, good heavens! It was gone!

"Where's my bag?" I shouted fiercely at the poor passengers with accusing eyes. "The man that got off took it," said one honest-looking little countryman. "Was it yours?" he asked.

"What, that man... his ticket was for Rome: the inspector told him it was better to change at Salerno!" I dashed out into the corridor.

Frantically, from one carriage to another, wild with rage, I hunted for him. It didn't seem possible to me that he had got off the train, just as the theft didn't seem possible or credible. I could get no peace: up and down the carriages four or five times, knocking on closed doors of toilets that were soon shut in my face. At last, after knocking at one of them for a while and getting no reply, I shouted: "Come out, you coward! Come out!"

When at length the door opened, there appeared a terrified little boy of seven or eight, his face and hands stained with chocolate. Bursting into helpless tears he ran off down the corridor.

I went inside and gaped speechless at the mess; Mrs Profetti's package, sewn into a piece of cloth, had been ripped open and the chocolate, obviously melted by the heat, had become stuck to books, socks and handkerchiefs, while a jar of honey had got broken. On the floor lay the bread, the half-eaten sausage and my poor garments, all soiled and unrecognisable. The flask of wine and my shaving things were missing. I thrust the lot, all mixed up, into the knapsack, opened the door to go back to my compartment, when... Ah! There you are!... Face to face with the miscreant.

A chill shudder went through me. First he started to run unsteadily towards the rear of the train. I dropped the knapsack and went after him. I could have strangled him: But when I got to the rear-end, a few yards from the last door, I stopped, unable to move. The villain, his back to the door, had pulled out a long knife. All I could do was to stare him out, try to make him lower his eyes. In them, red with terror and stupefied with wine, I could see the desperation of a trapped animal. This was no time to play the hero: slowly I backed away, keeping my eyes fixed on his; and still moving backwards, after picking up the bag I regained my compartment.

At Salerno, I saw him leave the train, but by then I had no further interest in him.

> Gente a cui fa notte avanti sera...
> non ti curar di lor ma guarda e passa.
>
> Dante

*

An old lady dressed in black, pale and ill-looking, who was going to see a specialist at Naples, kindly offered to stitch it for me. At any rate, I thought, it must have been in that state before it was stolen, and so I would avoid the explanation – and most of all the shame of the incident.

At five in the afternoon, after a journey of nine hours, we arrived at Naples central station, Partenopea. There street vendors, prostitutes and soldiers seeking ways of escape, were swarming in circles like moths around a naked light, harassing the passengers. Panders from the hotels offered tickets, addresses and introductions.

Having no preference I made for the Terminus Hotel believing it safe and dependable, and after getting fixed up with a room I went back to the station for information about trains to Caserta. There was one that evening, but I felt muzzy and needed rest; and there was another next morning at seven-forty.

After eating a pizza with a glass of wine and buying a couple of sandwiches and a bottle of mineral water, I went to bed. It was still daylight, not later than seven o'clock.

I slept as I hadn't slept for years and woke at four in the morning. Dressing immediately I paid my bill and made for the station.

There was already a long queue at the Caserta platform and by the time the train came in it was longer than ever. As usual; soldiers, prisoners of war and refugees returning home formed the great bulk the passengers. Compared with the train to Taranto this one was twice as crowded and I didn't manage to find a seat. I had to be content to stand and to rest my posterior occasionally on a wooden table in the middle of the compartment; it was a low table and the position was suffocating. When the train moved off I managed to get my head out of the window, and what I saw horrified me. Along the whole length of the side of the train on the steps of the coaches, stretched huge numbers of youths, boys and soldiers clinging precariously to the windows, their feet over the wheel springs. They were desperate to reach their goal, just as the unhappy salmon is powerfully urged back by nature to reach the source of its river.

Whistling and hooting repeatedly the train set off on its slow, lugubrious journey. Damaged bridges and unsafe embankments caused frequent stops.

The heat and smoke took the breath away, one's head reeled, and disgusting smells made one want to be sick.

On the map this place Caserta looked quite close to Naples, yet one never seemed to get there. The worst moment was when we came to a bridge; the train came to a stop, and an official went up and down it two or three times warning those clinging on to come down, since the temporary metal bridge was narrow and they would be crushed. But nobody seemed to want to know. Eventually he promised that the train would wait for them at the other end, whereupon they nearly all came down; only those standing right on the steps were unwilling to lose their places of vantage.

The train started off again; then, half way across the bridge, the disaster happened: two youngsters were crushed to death by the metal girders, struck down like migrating birds on their way to warmer Southern habitats but now too weak to keep up with the flock and dying even within sight of the lagoon they longed to reach.

One more interminable stop, this time in stunned silence.

It was nearly mid-day when we finally got to Caserta. I headed at once for Alberto's barracks, grateful for a light breeze and keener than ever to meet him, as though he really were my brother.

*

Strolling along the pavement looking this way and that, so as not to arrive at the barracks during meal-time, I was overtaken by a gig for hire drawn by a horse moving at a dejectedly slow pace. The horse was all skin and bone; solidified tears filled its eyes which were sleepy and drooping as if to indicate its complete indifference to the things of this world. The diminutive driver, who had boils, informed me that it was more than a mile to the barracks; and after we had haggled and wrangled over the fare, I got in. At all events there was no danger of my arriving too early with that poor horse which could scarcely stand up on its four spindly legs.

The broad highway which must have been the main street of the town was as desolate as the streets of Naples: people shouting and waving at each other from one vehicle or shop to another, while a great many others plodded along, pale, silent and aimless, walking only in order to mock at the enormous burden of their worries and anxieties.

At the gate of the barracks the horse stopped, needing no signal or word of command. I paid the fare and got out.

Slightly hesitant at the sight of the armed sentry standing stiff and stern at one side of the entrance, I approached and asked for Corporal Profetti. The sentry sprang forward and uttered a sharp bark which I understood to be the word "Sergeant". A sergeant emerged at once from a small hut just inside the gate, asked me who I was, who I wanted and why; then, satisfied with my answers, he gave me a sign to follow him.

So at last I was going to meet this paragon of intelligence, his mother's little darling and Sylvia's big brother. I had an almost feverish eagerness to know him, but this coming and going of 'enemy' soldiers on the soil of my native land, despite all my willingness to understand, accept and be resigned to the 'fait accompli', made my blood boil at the humiliation. I waited outside the big hut while they called him, and the moment I saw him come out there was no need for introductions: he was a perfect copy of his mother – the same olive complexion and fine big Tuscan nose which did not belie its origins.

I stepped forward eagerly to meet him with a bright, open smile, but I noticed at once a coolness and some irritation in the expression on his face. In different circumstances I would have stopped and adopted an attitude of mutual indifference; but after all the trials of that troublesome journey this seemed unwise, and I thought his coolness might dissolve: after all, if he resembled his mother there must be some good in him.

Persevering, I pressed on, hand outstretched, to give him a cordial embrace.

"You're Alberto, aren't you?"

"Yes," he replied, keeping me at a distance.

This wasn't very encouraging.

"I've come," I continued, "because your mother wanted me to bring you this package."

"Yes," he remarked, "she wrote to me about it. She could have sent it by post."

"Maybe she thought I was eager to meet you... or the other way round." This piece of irony struck home.

"Yes indeed," he said, smiling at last as he took the package. "Sorry!" Even though I had my doubts about all those attributes of Alberto that Mrs Profetti proclaimed, one thing, I thought, was true: his shyness. But I wasn't quite convinced. Yes, I said to myself, his shyness, but I knew deep down that I was seeking excuses for my disappointment.

Perhaps he would have preferred me just to hand over the package and go away. However, clearly embarrassed when I made no move, he asked:

"Shall we have a coffee?"

"Sure," I replied.

Despite the extreme vexation and disillusionment I felt at my futile, ill-considered journey, I was comforted by the realisation that I was enjoying the situation: I couldn't help putting on an odd smile that was perhaps ironical. Alberto was unworthy of my painstaking thoroughness, but I had done it for his mother's sake – which consoled me.

We made our way, without speaking, to the barracks' canteen or cafeteria. A dozen soldiers sitting at the small tables gave him a friendly greeting: "Hello, Al" – an obvious diminutive.

After we had found seats Alberto got up, went to the counter and soon returned with two coffees and some biscuits. Sitting down he took a penknife from his pocket and, shifting the package onto his knees from the chair he had left it on, began to undo the stitching.

His look of surprise was something I wouldn't have missed for worlds.

I had to remain calm and innocent-looking, even rather inattentive.

When he peered into the package his face contorted in a grimace and he looked up at me questioningly. The cloth container now resembled a handbag, and holding it open in his two hands he showed me the contents.

Gesturing at great length my surprise and repugnance, hands raised to high heaven, I indicated that it must have been the sun, the heat, and he agreed. Bursting into uncontrollable laughter he went over to a group of friends or fellow soldiers sitting nearby. Passing round the opened package from one to the other with witty remarks and loud guffaws, they all had an uproarious time.

In this way I discovered to my surprise that Alberto was not the shy, ingenuous person I had imagined, if he was capable of being drawn into such affability and merriment. So then? What was there between him and me that kept him so watchful and cautious – cold, wary as an owl, even downright rude?

My show of goodwill had served no purpose; the reason being that we have deep within us something called instinct which imposes upon us actions and attitudes deriving from our subconscious; these present a challenge to our goodwill and reject the precepts of education, religion and civil behaviour.

Thus there existed between Alberto and me a psychological barrier.

Among his army mates he was a British soldier, and outside the barracks one of the victors, tolerated and even respected. But in my presence his conscience was unconsciously aroused, placing upon him the burden of his origin, even though he bore no blame for that.

Perhaps he felt the lash of my contempt – now non-existent – which he imagined was still there?

My contempt?... Was it now non-existent?   Good intentions, understanding?... Very well, let them go.

Resentment?... Was it true that this also had been buried along with my good intentions?

No, it still smouldered, unknown to myself, and only Alberto could see it, intuitively.

I felt that I was more to blame than he was.

When he came back to our table I gave him a long, sad, troubled look and understood that the barrier dividing us could only be removed in the process of time.

The whole idea of the parcel and the journey had been an unhappy one.

"When are you leaving," he asked.

I was about to say "Tomorrow morning", but corrected myself.

"I'm not sure," I replied. He had in his hand a letter, apparently from inside the package, which I hadn't noticed.

"She tells me to give you a bar of chocolate," hesitating as he added dejectedly: "Just take the lot – if you can salvage anything."

"No thanks," I replied, "Sorry" – pointing to the sticky mess inside the package.

He accompanied me right to the gate, where we said goodbye. I am not sure whether he too had understood.

On my way to the station, dispirited and weary, I thought of the long journey I still had to make and of the night-long queue for the train.

When I finally got home I tumbled headlong into bed and slept for twenty-four hours, oblivious to everything.

A few days later I wrote to Mrs Profetti.

"Dear Mrs Profetti,

... I have met your boy Alberto and given him the package. I must say that he is exactly as you described him to me.

... He is in excellent health and often thinks of you both. Thank you again for all your kindnesses and affection. A warm embrace for you, dear Mrs Profetti, and... a fond kiss to Sylvia."

Dreaming of Mother

Four months in the training camp, most of it spent doing military exercises. Left, right, left, right!... About turn!... Platoon... Halt... Forward march!... Left, right, left, right!... Halt.

The platoon was a fine sight at the passing out parade and the battalion commander was praised and complimented by the Colonel.

Third battalion, Third Regiment of Tank Infantry. Apart from the officers and non-commissioned officers, we were all volunteers ranging in age from sixteen to eighteen. Some had already been promoted to Corporal. At the end of the passing out parade and after we had all sworn the Oath of Allegiance, we were permitted a short home leave, then it was straight to Naples for embarkation to Libya.

Anyone who has seen a herd of colts in a corral, could easily imagine the exuberance and joie de vivre of this Company of boys who, even though they were bound by military discipline, felt as if they had been liberated from the anxiety and the desperation of views without horizons which had forced them to enrol. Unemployed and without hope, most of them came from sleepy little villages and had taken the only road open to them towards any future, freeing themselves from the weight of inertia and abandonment in which the spirit suffocated and apathy spread a veil of ever-thickening fog, destroying ambition and closing the door to hope.

Most of them had left their homes as if abandoning a sinking ship and, having jumped, they had no idea of how cold the sea would be and how many would be able to reach a lifeboat.

A light-armoured tank battalion was made up of a limited number of men; the crews, the cooks, two motor cyclists, two medics, the admin office and the workshop. In all, less than a hundred and fifty men and, by now, we knew each other as though we had been together all our lives.

As usually happens though, small groups soon formed, brought together by ideas held in common or by convergent interests, temperament and mutual liking.

My group of friends was formed by two boys from Frosinone Province (the Ciociara people), two from Rome (the rascals), one from Molise and my friend Matteo, from my own village in Lucania.

The special train from Bologna to Naples made very few stops, speeding along as if late for an appointment. There were three coaches at the tail end of about ten goods wagons loaded with tanks and lorries. In the wide bends, the locomotive with its red-tinged plume of smoke, could be seen keenly climbing uphill or skidding slightly in the headlong descents. The dark shadows of the tanks absorbed with silent indifference the shafts of moonlight which bathed the peace of the hills, from whose slopes flickered the melancholy lights of sleepy villages. The brightly lit stations slipped behind us and on each of them we imprinted the echo of our songs. No one slept.

At about ten in the morning we arrived at Naples. Straight away we were embarked. A warm and caressing April sun spread a mantle of azure light over the slopes of Posillipo, and on our right the lovely coastline dotted with houses right down to Sorrento, was reflected on a deep blue, immobile and mysterious sea, while a pure white mist, like cotton wool, circled Vesuvius hiding its summit.

We were soon given breakfast consisting of coffee, rolls, butter, cheese and jam, sitting in well padded chairs in the large canteen. In the barracks at Bologna we had had to eat breakfast standing up, or sitting on low walls, the staircase, and sometimes, on rainy days, even in the toilets.

After breakfast, everyone went up on deck to admire the landscape. It was like the start of a cruise. Some played cards, some draughts or chess and some wrote the last letter from Italy. A group of soldiers started singing the famous Alpine song: "There, on those mountains... "

At dusk the big ship raised anchors and slowly moved away from the jetty, to the accompaniment of a military march played by the Bersaglieri band. The sun, disappearing towards Ischia, as though swallowed by the sea, left behind a bright orange sky in which some small clouds seemed to dip, absorbing colours.

The ship soon left the harbour and while Naples receded into the distance, it was lit by a million lights, throwing a dazzle into the sky. For a while, all the lads fell silent, overcome by the sadness of that parting.

On the high sea, the moon came out to flood the decks, leaving a long trembling strip of light on the black sea. The song, shouts and card games restarted as if the pause for nostalgic reflection had been nothing more than an involuntary break for prayer or a momentary pack of conscience at leaving the homeland. Youth was imposing itself with all its vigour.

The nearer we got to Africa the hotter the sun became. The lads were all using deck chairs to get a suntan, unaware of the kind of heat they would encounter in the desert. However, there was such joie de vivre in the air, an exhilarating first taste of pleasure and an almost childlike sense of adventure. Three days later we arrived at Tripoli : it was the 18th of April, 1940.

This time, the armoured cars which had been loaded after us in Naples, were off-loaded before us. We were still dressed in our winter uniforms, made from a grey-green heavy woollen material and were wearing long leather boots. The tanks and lorries moved off across the lovely square, heading for Porta Benito and the barracks at Azzizzia, where we arrived drenched in sweat and half suffocated.

Three days later we were the main participants in the 21st of April Parade, the tiny little tanks rolling merrily again through the flag-draped streets. For the first time we saw German officers on the saluting podium.

Germany was advancing on all fronts; in Austria, Czechoslovakia and in Poland. The Fascist propaganda presented these victories as ours, glorifying them in the press and on radio, ridiculing the scarecrow politicians of France, Britain and the United States, nations which, in the general opinion, would quickly surrender.

Everywhere there was a climate of hysterical exaltation in which the destruction of Warsaw, screened a thousand times in cinemas, was acclaimed with applause even louder than a performance at La Scala, Milan. The news of thousands of dead and injured was treated just like an arithmetical equation : grateful thanks was even given in churches.

We remained in Tripoli, in this climate of exaltation for little more than a month, after which the Battalion was transferred to the Oasis of Zuara, in preparation for our "walk into Tunisia".

*

At Zuara, we set camp near a large windmill beneath which a big reservoir serving irrigation channels, doubled as swimming pool. We all had a great time. In the cool of the evenings we played cards or told each other tales of our civilian life. The two Romans, Tarquinio and Vinicio, were mechanics by trade. Tarquinio worked alongside his father who was the proprietor of a repair workshop and Vinicio's father ran a bus. Gino's parents (the lad from the Ciociara), were farmers and owned vineyards. Giovanni, from Molise, worked in a restaurant with his father. All this had to be taken with a pinch of salt of course.

Tarquinio and Vinicio were the ones who told tall stories; every weekend, from their village some twenty miles away, they used to come to Rome with but one purpose in mind – amorous adventures. Their tales were spun with a typical Roman flamboyance. Gino often tried to drop in with some witty tale, but was immediately interrupted and shouted down by the Romans.

Vinicio was a tall, sunburnt chap, although not very solidly built. He was generally serious-minded, particularly when he was working on his engines. He was considered the best mechanic in the battalion but, when he was with Tarquinio, the two of them seemed intent on competing with each other for the greatest praise. In his serious moods Vinicio was a kind lad and I was glad that I liked him for his manliness and his frequent pieces of advice which, for his age, always seemed full of common sense.

Tarquinio was small but very robust. His moods varied from day to day and we were never sure whether he could be trusted. He had a dark, almost chocolate-brown complexion and eyes that became quite aggressive when he got excited either telling a joke or if he got angry during an argument. Occasionally he would also fall into a deep state of melancholy when he would go off by himself leaving his friends in anxiety.

Giovanni, from Molise, was a little overweight, not very tall and had a round face and calloused hands. He was undoubtedly a farmer's son, but he always said he helped his father in his own restaurant. Although we all understood that this could not be the truth, we gave him the benefit of the doubt.

I knew Matteo, the chap from my own village well, you might even say from birth. He was kind, serious, had a somewhat delicate constitution and was a loyal friend. He barely managed to raise a smile at the Roman boys' jokes and left no one in any doubt that he did not believe a single word of them. His obsession was a limitless hatred for the clergy, authority and the land-owning gentry: however instead of hitting out at them, he only grumbled and submitted, giving each their due respect. He and I hardly ever spoke to each other. Besides, he belonged to another unit so we rarely saw one another.

Tonino, the other lad from Frosinone, had become my closest friend. He listened to the Romans' stories and jokes open-mouthed, taking them in word for word as a parched man in the desert would drink a glass of cold water, laughing unrestrainedly.

He was so frail he seemed to be ill. He looked always tired and sleepy and anything he was told had to be repeated, he would suddenly jerk as though awakening from a dream. He was always full of fear and would tremble at the slightest noise, then, realising there was nothing to be scared of, he would smile wryly. Even when he walked, he moved jerkily on skinny legs which seemed hard put to maintain a straight line. His timidity had always attracted the attention of the arrogant bully who usually found easy prey in the weak, on whom they take out their cowardice.

I found him behind an armoured car one evening, crying.

"What's wrong," I asked worriedly.

Holding back his sobs, he dried his tears.

"Nothing," he replied.

"What do you mean nothing? Have you had bad news from home?"

"No."

"So, why are you crying?"

"I don't know. When I'm alone, I start thinking... "

"Thinking about what? You are just being silly," I said, trying to find an excuse for his weakness. "Get up," I continued. "Let's go for a walk and it will pass."

He got up slowly, keeping his head lowered. "I'm scared," he murmured.

"What of?" I asked.

"Of everything, of the war. If I have to go to the front, I'll die before I get there."

"Don't talk such rubbish!" I said resolutely.

"I should not have enlisted... they should not have taken me. Had it not been for that strong recommendation from my uncle, who is in the Recruiting Office, they would not have taken me."

"But you wanted to enlist, right? You were not forced, were you?"

"Forced?... Was I? What made me do it? Desperation, that's what! Desperation, that's why I did it."

I looked at him for a moment. By the light of a full moon already high in the sky, I saw two clear eyes and a proud expression which suddenly slid into anger.

"I'm sorry," he said quietly, "can you forgive me?"

"There's no need to apologise. I understand."

"You see," he continued, "my father was a teacher. He died five years ago. My mother is also a teacher, but she has asthma and suffers from arthritis. She has hardly been able to walk for the past seven years and more. I have two older sisters: one works at the Town Hall and the other looks after mother. We had some money put aside and some properties, but little by little we sold everything. Me?" he paused slightly, turning to look at me, "I'm a parasite."

"But... I am sure they love you... "

"Quite overpoweringly! I enlisted in secret; only my uncle was happy to see me go. When I left them, all three of them cried. 'Good heavens' my mother said through her tears, 'so frail... to be a soldier!'"

"My mother cried as well. All mothers cry when their sons leave home." I said.

"But... They always protected me! I had three mothers, you understand? Three mothers!" and he burst out crying again like a child.

I put an arm round his shoulders. " Leave it be. Think no more of it. Let's go back to the tent," I said. "I have a flagon of wine; all will be forgotten. You must not be afraid of anything," I said to encourage him.

From that moment, Tonino became my best friend. I loved him like a brother. He made me read letters from his mother, who continued to call him "My baby".

I had become his protector. He looked at me the way a puppy looks at its master. I sometimes felt embarrassed. When he was near me he felt at ease, he said, and strange as it may seem, I too felt at ease. His good manners and great goodness of spirit, earned him not only my affection, but a great respect as well.

We were in Zuara for just under three weeks. He and I were both in the repair shop, but we were not likely to stay there long due to illness among the tank crews. Together, we enlisted for a lorry driving course, but unfortunately Tonino failed the test and we were separated. I stayed on in the repair shop and Tonino was assigned to the tanks as a machine-gunner, imagine that! A sergeant squared him up and decided to make him get over his fears, which he did.

He was sent to another platoon but we were always together in our free time. He began to gain confidence in himself a little at a time, and soon he was able to strip down and reassemble the parts of the machine-gun. Returning from a firing exercise, he told me how he had hardly loaded the weapon when he began to tremble like a jelly. After shooting for a few minutes, though, he felt as if he had in his hands a toy which his father had given him many years ago for Befana, an old Italian custom similar to Christmas, where children receive toys on Twelfth Night. He told me that latterly, even his dreams had changed.

For a long time, he had been confiding in me that he awoke at night with a jerk, generally having dreamed of being kicked in the chest by a horse or of falling from a great height. "Sometimes now," he said, "I simply dream of my mother."

With the fall of France there was no longer any need to keep troops on the Tunisian front, so the units stationed there gradually began to be transferred to Cyrenaica. We knew our turn was approaching but, in the meantime we continued to enjoy the euphoria of victory, anticipating the early end of the war, expected perhaps even before our departure. The camp looked like a Boy Scouts' outing; there were songs and music to late hours. They had even stopped playing taps and the radio; between one patriotic song and another, they praised the high morale of the troops and the triumphs of Mussolini. One evening we saw bright flashes over Tripoli, followed by an immediate order to put off all lights. Once we got over the initial surprise, we stood watching with amusement and a little apprehension the spectacle of the anti-aircraft guns in the distance.

It was the first taste of contact with reality.

Even though in our hearts each of us was weighed down with his own fears, we had to keep them to ourselves looking as if we were ready to accept any possibility, even eventual encounters with the enemy, remote as it was made to look. No one believed it would come to that but ten days later came the order to strike camp and leave.

A great feeling of excitement ran throughout the camp. So much to do before leaving; test the engines, clean the weapons, take down the tents and fill the tanks with petrol; there was no time to think of anything else.

In the afternoon the big lorries arrived. One by one the tanks were loaded and camouflaged as well as possible with branches and palm fronds. About an hour before we departed, Tonino came to see me; he was trying hard to look calm and unworried.

"What do you think?" he asked me. "Will the British resist?"

"I am not sure," I replied. "It looks as if they are not going to surrender, but it will not last long."

"I had a letter from home this morning. They tell me my younger sister is engaged to be married. I know the chap, he is a good boy. I feel sorry for the older one, making sacrifices in order to stay with mother. They also sent me a beautiful Crucifix; have you got one?"

"I have got a medal of Saint Anthony."

"That is good," he said, reassured. Just then, the Sergeant called him back to his unit.

*

At about midnight the motorised column got on its way. No headlamps, but a big moon in a clear African sky shone like daylight. Out tanks looked even more insignificant on those big lorries, almost as though aware of their inadequacy. Sitting on top or standing at their sides, the crew: two lonely men, in the cold of the African night, like two phantoms standing still but moving all the same to an uncertain end, at the mercy of duty, at the service of Death.

When we got near Tripoli the anti-aircraft batteries and the searchlights began to pierce the sky again. A large flash erupted near the harbour; a bomb perhaps?

A while later calm was restored again under the big moon that seemed to be laughing derisively. We skirted the town in a hurry as if wishing to get away as quickly as possible from the dangers that lurked there, without thinking of the sights trained on us, just as ours were trained on the other side of the hedge.

We still had a long way to go. Our destination was rumoured to be Tobruk. The tank crews stretched themselves out on the platform beside the armoured cars and the side plank of the lorries and went to sleep, while the column sped on into the night without interruptions.

It was sunrise when we got to Sirte. In the East the sun was red, trembling in the morning mist, and in the South an orange-coloured accumulation of clouds announced the coming of a gibleh, the desert wind. Already a warm breeze was blowing through the palms.

The canteen lorry which had left the camp the previous afternoon, had set up under a group of palms close to a wind-turned well. A delicious smell of coffee emanating from the steaming pots saturated the air.

The irresistible appeal of a good meal after such a long journey tempted us to run towards it, but roll-call was announced from the Command vehicle and at the same time the workshop Sergeant called us, saying the mechanics were excused roll-call because we had to effect urgent repairs to some of the lorries.

With Vinicio, one of the Roman mechanics, we went to the rear of the column where a lorry was losing oil from the sump. We set to work with a will so as not to miss breakfast, but ten minutes later we were called back to the Command vehicle where the muster had been prepared.

Lieutenant Salerno had the list of names in his hands and as soon as we got there he began the roll again. When he reached the letter "D" and Tonino's name, no one answered. Four times he shouted "Antonino De Piero... De Piero!" No one answered.

I could not believe it! Where was he hiding?... I began to get a bit concerned. I had not seen him since we left Zuara. I really ought to have popped in to see him before leaving Tripoli, if for no other reason than to make sure he was cheerful enough. However, knowing he had adapted well and seemed quite at ease for a bit, I felt not unduly worried.

They pulled the driver of the tank in which he manned the machine-gun out of the breakfast queue. When he was questioned, he shrugged his shoulders.

When roll-call was over, the trumpet-call to breakfast sounded from the Mess. I did not know what to think, so shaken with worry I joined the line and I was just about to pick my coffee up when loud screams and frantic sounds of running footsteps were heard. Soldiers were running towards one of the lorries. We left the queue and began running in that direction. Many soldiers had already gathered and a murmur was running from mouth to mouth. "De Piero... De Piero..." An Officer was shouting: "Get out of the way... get away you lot... call the assembly!"

Trembling I pushed my way through the crowd. I glanced along the side of the tank and for a while I was left petrified. My knees buckled and I fell in the sand. When I came to, a Medic was giving me a glass of water. There was only the Captain, the Lieutenant and the Medic.

"Was he a relative of yours?" asked the Lieutenant.

I tried to answer but I burst into tears, just like a baby. Not a syllable could I utter. Tonino was lying there pale and unmoving between the armoured car and the bank, the tank track barely touching his temple; the cursed tank track!... There was no sign of any blood.

His face was turned to the heavens, his eyes closed and his mouth set in a wide smile. It seemed as if death found him dreaming; dreaming of his mother. We departed and left him at Sirte... Without a medal... Without a flower...

The Man from Matera

As an emotional reaction to the perception of extraordinary facts and happenings our sense of wonder has, in the last half century, been subject to a decisive reverse in popularity. We no longer marvel at any strange little happenings. Nowadays, we need to witness real natural or scientific miracles just to experience a proper reaction of wonderment.

These small uncomplicated excitements have given way to a blasé attitude, except perhaps if an atom bomb is dropped or if an astronaut lands on the moon.

We are left in a sort of stupor as, through the increasing speed of communications, we are made aware that our planet is nothing but a small ball of earth and rocks wandering through the immensity of space, so that we often consider ourselves neighbours, but neighbours who occasionally hate or even kill each other.

Indeed the world has been made to look quite small.

That it is small is confirmed by the ease with which one can travel from one end of the earth to the other and the common occurrence of meeting the man next door or a school friend of twenty or thirty years ago in the densest of human jungles, such as New York, Paris, London or Tokyo. This is perhaps the reason why my meeting with this old acquaintance would have been nothing more or less than a normal happening, had it not been for the manner, the circumstances and the place of that meeting, and the discovery of a continuity in his peculiar character and style, a consequence of his Adonis-like physique, destined to attract women and then come to grief with them.

We met each other again on some remote offshore island, inhabited by all sorts of birds and seals in the far north-west of Scotland. Call it a strange coincidence if you will, but one wonders what kind of amused and capricious hand was at work to bring us together again in this far away corner of our little planet after more than thirty years. The hand of Venus or some other God of beauty and virility perhaps, evoking images of Matera within the pages of this short story and reviving memories and romantic deeds which are never really lost with the march of time? These past events, quite possibly, left living proof of his prowess, if all the tales of romance and adventure he told me were true and captivated me in my early adolescence, that time of my life when I could still be amazed by little miracles.

I was about fifteen then and attending the secondary school in Matera, about thirty miles from my native village, when I first met this "dandy"; he was twenty. A lot of water has passed under the bridge since then. My name is Frank Rossi, one of literally thousands of Rossis in Italy. I have lived in Glasgow for the last thirty years where I run a small cafe.

The circumstances that found me in these remote islands can be attributed partly to my curiosity and partly to my esteem for and friendly attitude towards the people of this hospitable nation: I could no longer bear the rebukes of my Scottish friends and trade representatives who came into my shop socially or on business.

"Mr Rossi, how are you?... I have just returned from a trip to the Highlands... the scenery is fantastic... Have you never been there?"

"Good Morning, Mr Rossi, I am just back from the Shetland Islands, a beautiful place... Have you never been there?... What a pity... I am surprised; you should go sometime."

They made me feel guilty for not being able to appreciate the beauty of their country. So, since I was going to have some free time to myself, I decided to put an end to the embarrassing situation and bought a ticket for a three-day guided tour of the Western Isles.

At that time, I used to put birds along with most other animals. But I know so much about them now that I have come to admire them and wonder at their ability to escape the earth's gravity that keeps us poor bi-peds stuck on the ground. Suddenly to discover, on getting aboard the coach, that the tour had been organised by an Association of Ornithologists made me feel silly. I should really have checked the programme and not just the itinerary. However, in the end I was not disappointed.

There were other people on the tour who had nothing to do with the study of flying creatures: a newly-wed French couple on honeymoon, interested only in themselves, a few Japanese tourists.

What was strange and unusual was the fact that, whether by coincidence or design, this old friend of mine should have chosen the same trip as me. As far as I knew, neither he, nor his partner were of the type to take up ornithology.

Our meeting must therefore have been arranged by destiny or some superior being.

*

When the two of them arrived at the starting point for the trip, in front of the travel agency, most of the passengers were already in their seats on the coach. A cigar-coloured Rolls Royce, chauffeur-driven and possibly hired, stopped just in front of the coach causing heads to turn. Everyone stopped talking, myself included, and with wide-eyed curiosity and stretching of necks, we all tried to see what was happening.

When we saw the Tour Guide, dressed in the agency uniform, rushing to the car, we knew the occupants were coming with us.

First to alight was the man. He ceremoniously offered his hand to the lady, helping her out of the car. She had a round face set off by a large pair of pink-framed spectacles. She was unashamedly dressed in a wide variety of bright colours; a lime skirt topped by a mauve blouse, an orange overcoat and a blue hat covered with Bird of Paradise feathers. She was quite stout, but solid and well-built, as is common in people who are well fed. She looked the personification of opulence. Her feet were tiny for her size and she wore a pair of grey-coloured crocodile shoes. She had on a lot of jewellery; two or three large rings on her chubby little fingers, broaches and a pearl necklace. Beneath those glasses were a pair of bright eyes. A translucent pink lipstick had been applied quite-generously to her fleshy lips.

The gentleman who was with her looked like one of those posters that used to advertise the Charleston in the twenties. He was tall, elegantly dressed in a grey silk suit, a waistcoat with buttons covered with the same material, patent leather shoes and the whitest of shirts against which a turquoise blue tie looked most handsome. In his buttonhole he wore a small tea rose.

He was much younger than the lady, perhaps fifty or so. His dry, fresh complexion and his proud composure indicated a man accustomed to being admired. His hair was black and slightly greying at the temples; he had cold, black, still and staring eyes, an aquiline nose and thin lips which terminated in two little dimples on the side of his mouth. Had he been naked, I am sure he would have looked like one of those Greek statues to be found in most museums. The physical disparity between the two was odder than their clothes.

When the couple started climbing the steps up into the vehicle, all the passengers rushed to their seats and, apart from some disparaging comments of "Americans" from the back seats, no one else uttered a single word about them. Everyone suddenly looked as though their curiosity had been fully satisfied, and so it continued for the rest of the trip.

The strange couple made themselves comfortable on two seats in front of me. Apart from the disparities in their appearance they could easily have been taken for a married couple on honeymoon. But when the man helped the lady to alight and let her pass in front of him with a courteous bow I noticed a sort of grin on his face, as though he were distancing himself from the scene.

Just at that moment our eyes met.

He looked at me with a guilty start, as if he feared being recognised and went on doing so throughout the journey, much to my annoyance and discomfort. After some time I began to be aware that his face reminded me of something, somebody, or perhaps an episode in my life which I couldn't place. I soon put aside this idea, ascribing it to the gentleman's unusual behaviour in continually staring at me, although his face gradually seemed more and more familiar.

I tried hard to show indifference. I was ably helped in this by my neighbour, a man of about forty who was quite tall and slim with a sort of giraffe-like neck. He sat erect and stiff in his seat, so much so that when he stood up and walked in the corridor, I am sorry to say I kept mentally placing a ruler on his back noting how his neck, shoulders, back and his bottom held a perfect perpendicular position as if held in place by a rod.

After introducing himself as Mr George Jones, from Yorkshire, this gentleman began talking about birds with an infantile enthusiasm. Hard as I tried, I was completely unable to make him change the subject. He listed them all, describing to me every feature of a dozen species of gulls, and ended by stating convincingly that on a small island, the one he hoped we were going to visit, there was a pair of royal eagles blown there by a gale from the Rocky Mountains of Canada. More than once I thought of changing my seat, but I resisted the temptation and went on suffering the lessons in ornithology with only an occasional yawn.

Thankfully, the tour guide broke the monotony at intervals by pointing out the natural beauties encountered during the journey, adding historical comments, anecdotes and a few jokes, at which the American lady laughed her head off.

There was a brief stop at Stirling Castle, and then we went off to Inverness through a profusion of forests and along the banks of countless lochs. When we got to Loch Ness, the guide commented on its depth; nearly three hundred metres she said. She added that it was home to a big monster called Nessie who lived at the very bottom and who, now and then, surfaced to the great excitement of those who spotted it. A sizeable Japanese expedition had searched for it at length with ultra-modem equipment and while they had been unable to find it, they had recorded some strange loud sounds thought to come from the monster.

There was another short stop at Blair Castle, where the Laird is Commander-in-Chief of his own private army made up of workers employed on his estate. The men are dressed in the uniform of the castle clan and they carry ancient muskets and knives, and wear sporrans.

We passed quite near a spot where, the guide said, a large number of Scots women and children had been slaughtered by the English in a bloody battle. The place was very dreary and silent. Culloden was the name. A short while later we reached Inverness where we stopped for lunch in one of the Town's large hotels.

Alighting from the coach I heaved a great sigh of relief, thinking I had finally got rid of my companions at least for the present. Alas it was not to be. The American gentleman would not give up. He continued to annoy me with his staring and I almost felt that he was afraid of me. He kept making a great fuss and being very formal to the lady while she was searching for a suitable table. Finally, they both sat across the room at a table within a large bay window just opposite me. To my great relief she contrived to place her companion with his back to me.

Meeting my gaze, the lady gave me a wry smile and soon began attacking the slice of melon and Parma ham.

With my napkin in my hand and my cutlery ready to start eating, I glanced around the dining room. I had completely forgotten my neighbour, Mr Jones, when I saw him coming out of a door down the corridor, the toilet perhaps. I turned away pretending I had not seen him, but it was to no avail. He came directly to an empty seat at my table, beside another middle-aged gentleman who sat in front of me without saying a word. It goes without saying that he ruined my appetite.

From Inverness, we passed through Dingwall and the road became quite bumpy. There were a few straight stretches, but also a lot of bends. On one side there was a river or some deep green lakes, on the other, wild mountains almost devoid of trees, nature at its primordial best. For over twenty miles there was just open countryside dotted with the odd cottage here and there but, as the sun went in and out of the clouds, the colours of the heather became brilliant: from bronze to mauve and pink, to black where autumn laid its cold hand on the heather blossoms. Here and there, groups of deer grazed peacefully. I do not think I have ever seen a more unspoiled natural environment. It drew lavish comments and praise from everyone, including my companion, and this thankfully gave me some respite from the lessons about birds. Even the American lady was captivated and she frequently uttered the word "marvellous" in open-mouthed astonishment. Taking advantage of her distraction, her companion turned to me with a broad smile.

I felt as though I had been struck by a bolt of lightning. Is it him?... Is it possible?

I was quite sure it was him, but it was so hard to believe. If it were him, what was his name? I tried unsuccessfully to find an answer.

This time he realised that I knew. He nodded to me and gave me another smile. Why, then, had he shown so much restraint and reserve? If he had recognised me right away why was he so cautious? Was he, perhaps, afraid of his wife? Indeed, was she his wife? This was another intriguing puzzle and just as mysterious.

Late in the afternoon, after several more stops and lectures from the guide on the history of Scotland, beginning with the Picts, who were the very early inhabitants, followed by the Viking raids and the Clan battles, we reached the little harbour town of Ullapool. We would sail from here the following morning for Stornoway, on the Isle of Lewis. We were all placed in various hotels or boarding houses. I was given accommodation, along with a dozen of my fellow travellers, including the American couple, in a very quaint hotel. It was decorated in the baronial style, complete with hunting trophies on the walls, and was some two hundred metres from the pier.

Having had more time to study his face, I was no longer in any doubt; it was him, that same Don Giovanni I had known in Matera when I was fifteen.

It surprised me that he had made no further efforts to reveal his identify. He did not say a word to me and I knew that, by now, he realised that I had recognised him.

*

The journey had made me quite tired, so I went straight up to my room for a rest. I had been trying hard to fall asleep for some time, but my mind kept wandering back in time to our days in Matera. Try as I might, I still could not remember the name of this man who had been the object of my admiration during my adolescent years.

In that somnolent state between waking and dreaming I began to reminisce, and found myself transported to a dingy boarding-house room less than fifty metres from the brightly lit Hotel Italia. The house was at the top of a street that ran steeply downhill, underneath an arch beneath some small houses, and right down to the Gravina through a maze of caves and surface dwellings called the Sasso and more particularly the Sasso Caveoso. The large oppressive structure of the cathedral bell tower, which looked as if it could crush all the little houses to rubble at any time, dominated every corner of my little room. On the balcony, the reflection from the hot white sandstone cliff across the stream was quite unbearable at times.

The blinding light from the prehistoric wall of solidified mollusc shells seemed to boil in the hot sun, sucking up the very air from the depths of the canyon-like ravine, where even the little greenery in the occasional roof garden was desiccated and brown. The houses were all painted white to reflect the heat, an odd tree had managed to survive somehow; the wind was completely still and sultry.

In the courtyards outside the caves many carts pointed their shafts at the sky as though begging for pity, and at night the tired lights, weighed down by the humidity, shone through the white smoke coming from small fireplaces.

A teeming life of quiet, unrelenting hardship went on in those labyrinths; a life totally different from that in the new part of town, where the bureaucrats, shopkeepers and the idle rich lived la dolce vita fanned by cool breezes.

Life in the Sasso, inhabited by the peasants for the most part, began at five in the morning when they hitched the mules to their carts and trundled off to work in the distant wheat fields, to the accompaniment of ringing wheels, the crack of whips and the clip-clop of hooves striking the wet, black asphalt. Wrapped in coats and blankets, the women and children tried to snatch a few more moments of sleep, as their menfolk drove the carts towards Montescaglioso and the Bradano river in a long trembling line of moving oil-lamps.

*

I was only fifteen then. Things, people, happenings around me all had an air of romance. Life was a joy and, if there was anything that disturbed my peace of mind more than anything else, it was the boldness of my so-called "friend", who would suddenly pop up in a mysterious, not to say suspicious way.

This "friend" of mine was at least five years older than me, as he had already served his time in the army. I could never understand why, of all the people his age and older he had to choose me for company and to tell his tales to. He was usually to be found in the main street of the town, especially in the evening when the "parading" started.

Tall, dry and faultlessly dressed, he stood above the crowd dominating it with his regal bearing. With the coolness of a hunting tiger his eagle eyes, black, still and impenetrable and framed by bushy eyebrows, roamed hither and thither over the "unsuspecting" ladies. His aquiline nose, under which there was the merest hint of a black moustache, stood above a thin and sinuous mouth. As I said, he was the personification of a Greek god.

He smoked very little but, as was common at the time, he carried a long cigarette-holder at shoulder height between his two middle fingers in a way that displayed a slim, delicate hand which had certainly never done a hard day's work in its life: in other words he was elegant.

I admired him yet I disliked him at the same time. Indeed, I think I hated him because I was small and very shy, not elegant or vain. He therefore took great pleasure in making me feel that way. His tales of daring escapades and romantic adventures left me open-mouthed. Nearly every evening at the same time, he would stop me in the middle of the main-street "parade" and inform me that he had an assignation with a lady-friend that evening, and would recount the deeds of the night before. It was as if he lived the adventures and I was destined to dream about them.

Even though I had no hope of emulating him, I went walking up and down the main street myself amid the bright lights and the scent of many perfumed ladies. A certain young girl of about twelve or thirteen kept buzzing around me like a bee. I told him she was my girlfriend and he gave me advice on how to make her mine. One evening, during the usual promenade from the public park to the Hotel Italia, I managed to slip a note into her hand: "You are beautiful; I love you."

Next day, after school, one of her young friends stopped me in the street and handed me a note on which there was just the one word: "Idiot!" On another occasion, during a celebration at the castle, I tried to take her hand. I should never have done it! She ran off downhill at breakneck speed, past boulders and rocks, leaving me feeling like some kind of monster. In those days, you see, young girls did not generally lose their innocence quite as readily as they do nowadays. There was no such thing as sex education in schools. And so I discovered that his lessons in gallantry did not work.

Soon after this disappointment of mine and after passing me in the street on several occasions, he stopped me once more, recounting his tales. He had actually slept with most of the beautiful women in the town; the wife of this big Fascist dignitary, the daughter of that lawyer and the wives of this doctor and that. There was also a widow I shan't name who had given him a lot of money.

He never worked, nor had I ever asked him about his parents or whether he had brothers and sisters. I never even knew where he lived. He was not a friend in the true sense of the word, he was just someone who confided in me all those marvellous tales which generated great admiration in me and, admittedly, a certain envy and jealousy.

A gong ringing somewhere in the house brought me back to reality: dinner was ready. I looked at myself searchingly in the mirror. Well, I mused, I am certainly not handsome nor dashing, but I am not unhappy. Maybe it is just as well that I am not like him.

After dinner and short walk to admire the view across the Loch towards Binn Ghablach, which stood solitary and black under a menacing umbrella of dark clouds everyone retired for the night, including the American lady and the gentleman who still appeared to have no intention of revealing his identity.

*

The following day, after breakfast the whole party made for the pier where a small ferry, which at first sight was of doubtful seaworthiness, was waiting for us. The crew were loading all sorts of merchandise on to it: machinery, a van, sheep and a horse. There was also a mad bull, who absolutely refused to cross the bridge. Finally they passed a broad leather strap under his stomach and hoisted him on board, still protesting loudly.

Contrary to our vile suspicions, the ferry sailed out of the harbour at full speed on a calm sea, hardly touched by the long and imperceptible swell of the waves, getting further and further away from the narrow delta into the open sea and leaving behind a landscape clad in heather and bracken. It was about eleven in the morning when we finally reached Stornoway, the capital of the Western Isles. A coach was waiting to take us to a small beach where we would board the fishing boats for the final leg of the journey to the bird sanctuary. Our guide said we were lucky to have such good weather, because these waters are usually very rough and the wind very fierce. There were a few trees around, but they were bent almost parallel to the ground by the constant force of the wind. We all crowded on to the fishing boat and set off for the bird sanctuary.

On reaching the island, the spectacle that greeted us was incredible. The rocks of the cliff rose perpendicular from the sea and perched on the very edges were the nests of millions of seabirds of all species: gulls, puffins, guillemots and others, to the delight of Mr Jones and the other bird-watchers. There were also a few seals and someone even spotted a whale. It was on the boat that the ice was finally broken, although personally, I felt I should have awaited our return to Stornoway.

A heavy swell suddenly made the American lady lose her balance and she stumbled and almost fell into my arms. He rushed to her side in concern while the lady, pale with fear at her narrow escape, thanked me effusively for helping her. Suddenly, and without thinking, I turned to the gentleman and said "I am sorry, but I seem to think I know you from somewhere."

"Of course you know me," he answered calmly. "And I know you."

We shook hands.

"Matera, remember?"

"Yes, that's it. Quite a long time ago, I am sure."

The American lady interrupted: "Do you two know each other?"

"Oh yes, when we were very young," I replied. "I am very sorry, but I cannot remember your name," I said, turning to him.

"Savino. Savino Verini. Yours I think was... "

"Franco."

"That's it," he replied. "Little Franco Rossi, right?"

"Very good," I said. "Your memory is certainly better than mine. I admired you very much, you know."

The American lady did not look terribly pleased and, a little grudgingly perhaps, she said: "Since you two know each other so well, perhaps we could have dinner together when we return to the mainland."

"Thank you," I replied. "I would be delighted to accept," and I discreetly moved away.

At about four in the afternoon we embarked on the little ferry for Ullapool, after a flock of sheep, pigs, chickens and some machinery had all been loaded for the return journey to the mainland. A threatening westerly wind had sprung up and the gathering low black cloud promised that the crossing would be decidedly stormy. As soon as we reached the open sea out of the shelter of the harbour, the wind began to lash the waves, making the sea boil and the little ferry toss like a cork. All the passengers were seated in the stern, protected by a wide glass screen. The noise of screeching steel and the force of the waves on the sides of the vessel, mixed with the cackle of the animals was terrifying. Some of the passengers were seasick while others, mostly the women, were all praying silently. However, the little ship continued to plough through the waves with proud indifference, as though she had seen it all before.

At about nine in the evening we arrived back in Ullapool and, even though it was summer and the daylight normally lasts until 11 p.m., the street lights were all lit; rain and low cloud hung over everything turning day into night.

An hour later we were served dinner in a well-lit corner of the dining room. The American lady ordered a shellfish starter, followed by a fresh salmon salad and, to finish, pineapple rings fried in bechamel sauce and served with fresh cream. She drank Chablis with the meal and the three of us finished with coffee and a Drambuie.

Throughout the meal Savino Verini was very nervous and uneasy. Perhaps he was afraid that I might say something indiscreet but, even if I had felt so inclined, I would have had little chance to do so. The lady, whom I now knew to be Edna Franklin, hardly closed her mouth for an instant. She either ate, or talked on a wide variety of subjects but never once, to my surprise, did she reveal anything about her private life. Savino and I had nothing to do but agree or disagree with what she said. About herself, she said only that her ancestors had come from Scotland and that she lived in New York. She talked about her jewels, her passion for horses, her travels to the Far East and of Chinese cuisine which was her favourite; never a word about her relationship with Savino.

When we rose from the table I offered to pay for the meal, but she would not hear of it and insisted that she would pay. We wished each other goodnight and the two of them retired to their room.

For my part, I was still curious about the relationship between the two of them and certainly none the wiser after our meal together. I went to the bar, ordered a whisky and took it to a small, round table. I was just hoping that Mr Jones, who was sitting with the French couple, would not get up and join me when I spotted Savino coming towards me.

He sat down and I offered to buy him a drink. He had a whisky and lemonade. We talked generally for a while and then I began to turn the conversation to his American companion.

"So," I asked suddenly, "what, if anything, can you tell me?"

"I know you must be curious about a lot of things," he said, smiling.

"I cannot deny it," I replied, "but if you would rather not say anything about your business or your life, you don't have to. We can talk of Matera instead."

"The lady, you see... " He paused for a while.

"... is you wife?" I suggested naively.

"Oh, no!" he said decisively.

"You do not need to go on." I said.

"No, it would not be right," he said with a wry smile.

By now I was anxious to learn more. "Well," I said in a manner which I hoped would encourage him to talk. Savino began to speak, slowly and timidly at first, but then with increasing confidence.

"As you probably guessed, the lady is not my wife. I am only telling you this and about my life because I do not want you to think me a coward for the second time."

"The second time? How come?" I asked in surprise.

"The lady is more than fifteen years older than me, and there would be only one reason for me to marry her: money."

"That would make no difference to me," I reassured him quickly.

"You would still think me a coward," he continued. "Do you remember what I once did in Matera?"

"No, I do not."

"I got married, remember?"

I let my mind drift back to that time in Matera and, sure enough, I did remember.

"A girl from Matera who was living in New York."

"That's right. She was also fifteen years older than me. I only did it so that I could emigrate to America. It was a tragedy: her brother nearly knifed me to death. In the end we divorced."

"Oh, I am very sorry." What else could I say, I was absolutely lost for words.

"I decided then that I would never marry again," he said firmly.

"So," I said encouragingly, as I felt some encouragement was needed.

"So," he went on, "since then I have lived 'la dolce vita'. I have travelled all over the world: from South America to Japan and from Australia to the South Seas and China."

By this time, Savino was well into his Matera act with exactly the same cunning and zeal. This time, though, he had the opposite effect on me. I suddenly felt very sorry for him.

"How did you manage that," I asked naively.

"After a few years of working as a waiter in a restaurant, I had a brilliant idea: to be a companion to those rich, old widows who are in need of distraction. I must say, I made quite a name for myself."

After a second and third whisky, Savino was beginning to get quite excited. "Everything is quite legal, of course," he said. "Strict rules are laid down and must be observed. I do not want to boast, but my reputation at the escort agency is quite high and there is a list of women who are waiting for my services. They trust me and I have never cheated any of them. In fact, my reputation at the agency is now so good that they allow me to choose the women I escort. "

I was both flabbergasted and amused. It showed on my face in a wry smile.

"You are laughing at me," he retorted. "But let me tell you that, at my age I try to avoid the younger women: they make too many demands on you. I prefer a quieter life now. Mrs Franklin, the lady I am escorting now, is no longer young. By this time of night she has taken a sleeping pill and gone to bed, where she will sleep until eight o'clock in the morning. In the evenings, therefore, I am free to do as I please. They pay me well for this, you know. In a few years I will have a lovely house on the Pacific coast."

"With a pretty little lady in it," I remarked just for something to say.

"Possibly," he replied. "And what have you been doing with yourself?"

I told him a little of what I had done: that I now lived in Scotland and that he could come and visit me if he liked. He therefore felt obliged to invite me to visit him at his home in Philadelphia.

He went on to say that the lady was not pleased if he left her alone during the day and that she liked people to think that he was her husband. He also told me that the women he escorted travelled legally on false passports acquired by the agency. They were coded in a certain way that would identify them to the police and their escorts would not then be open to possible blackmail. After a final drink when closing time was called, we wished each other goodnight and went to our rooms.

The return journey was much the same as the journey out: a few sidelong looks of recognition and a few smiles. When I met the lady occasionally, she greeted me by name: "Good morning, Mr Rossi," and I would reply: "Good morning, Mrs Franklin." She would not leave Savino's side for an instant, however. For his part, Savino played the role of husband with laudable style and composure.

Meanwhile, Mr Jones had returned to sit beside me. This time I was glad of his presence since he stopped me glancing, even involuntarily, at the unlikely couple and also running the risk of being a nuisance. Mr Jones began to tell me of some of the interesting people in our party: Professor Smith and Dr Jones, both famous ornithologists. Finally he asked me about the strange couple. I told him I only knew them to be American.

We stopped for tea at a small hotel in Pitlochry, on the shores of a small loch whose waters were of the deepest green imaginable and whose surface shimmered in a thousand reflections. We were then taken up to the dam where Mr Jones struck up an instant friendship with Mrs Franklin. All four of us then went up to see the salmon ladder. Mr Jones, who seemed to know as much about fish as he did about birds, explained that when they built the dam it would have been impossible for the salmon to get upstream to spawn. Therefore they had built this ladder comprised of forty large tanks into which the water cascaded from above and through which the salmon climbed to get to the higher reaches of the river. After laying their eggs, the salmon died.

Mrs Franklin found this upsetting but Mr Jones pointed out that when the eggs hatch in their millions, they immediately fall prey to a variety of predators, and those that survive begin making their way back down the river to the sea. By the time they get to the dam they are already some thirty centimetres long, and they return to the rivers of their birth only to lay their own eggs after three years in the open sea. Perhaps only one in a hundred thousand makes it back, but they each lay upwards of one hundred thousand eggs, thus completing the natural cycle once again.

Mrs Franklin listened with great interest, but she was not the type to encourage familiarity. So, with long acquired tact, she and her companion moved off.

Back at the coach depot, where we all said our goodbyes, I once again invited my "friend" Savino to come and visit me. He, too, renewed his invitation to me to visit him in Philadelphia.

But I never saw them again: the lady for obvious reasons and the man, due to an event as foreseeable as it was tragic.

A year or so after our meeting I took advantage of a special fare offer and flew to the United States. Remembering Savino's invitation, I decided to surprise him by going to visit him in Philadelphia. His house was in a neat suburb of the town, among grass verges and trees. I discreetly rang the bell and waited, slightly apprehensive at the thought of seeing my friend again. Some time later a dark woman in her sixties opened the door. As soon as she saw me, she began to cry.

"What is it?" I asked. "Did I startle you?"

She stopped crying and dried her eyes. "You are not the police, are you?" she asked as she let me in. "You are looking for Savino, no doubt. Poor Savino! I had to go and identify him, you know. Poor—!"

"What happened?" I asked, sensing the worst.

"Oh God! You do not know?... He fell from a balcony... a fiftyfloor balcony. What a terrible night that was... Poor Savino!"

Fell from a balcony? Savino fell from a balcony? Suddenly memories came back of a day, long ago in Matera, when I had seen him limping. He told me he had had to jump from a balcony and had ruined a good pair of trousers into the bargain.

I left the old lady still in a distressed state.

"The leopard doesn't change its spots, Savino falling from a balcony? More likely pushed by a jealous husband," I thought wryly.

That is how I came to write this story. I am sure there will still be people in Matera who remember him, and there will surely be many women, now middle-aged, who will lament his passing with sadness, wiping a nostalgic tear from their eyes. While some of their daughters, who never knew him, will ask their mothers for the umpteenth time: "Mama, am I really like father? I don't really think I am, you know."

Pax Vobiscum

In that little village in the mountains of Garfagnana, dominated by the imposing mass of the bell tower and stuck to the rock face as if held there by glue, they still remembered him as Uncle Romualdo even if they were nephews of three or four generations.

The forest o oak and chestnut reached right down from the mountain almost strangling the little village which still managed to gleam like a jewel when caught by the sun's rays.

This is where Uncle Romualdo was born.

They knew him by no other title or name and what they knew about him was only what their next of kin used to say about him;

"He was such a fine generous man!"

He had not been seen in the village for years and, except for an occasional letter to his old sister, just to say that he was well, nothing else was known about him.

Then, one day, following a long silence, came the dreaded news; it was brought to the village by an expatriate villager home on holiday.

Poor Uncle Romualdo!... They had a Mass said for him in the local church for the repose of his soul!

Uncle Romualdo had six brothers and three sisters. Only one was still alive. She was a woman of about eighty, weighted down by hardship and full of aches and pains. She took the news quite calmly; after such a long time away, it had seemed as if her brother no longer existed.

"Romualdo?... Is he dead?... He was a good man." That's all she could say.

Most of his brothers and sisters had left the village; some had to go to America, some to Australia and some to France. Romualdo and a sister had landed in Scotland.

Their father was a cobbler. People said that he was a good man but the sight of all those children on the poverty line had driven him to drink more than it was good for him. No one starved though thanks to those generous chestnut trees. The two-roomed house which served as habitat and workshop had a huge smoky fireplace where a large black pot hung from a soot-covered chain over a meagre fire.

The huge pot was always boiling chestnuts or wild vegetables. There were chestnuts everywhere in the house: chestnuts in the wardrobe, chestnuts in the drawers, chestnuts in sacks of all sorts and finally, piled in a corner against the wall. The children had them roasted, boiled, or made into a pudding with chestnut flour, any time of the day.

Sundays, however, were very special days; they longed for Sunday all through the week. On Sundays there was a treat for everyone: bread. They all sat around the table and on stools here and there while their father with a large loaf and a knife would go around giving everyone a slice that tasted like heaven.

"I can see you and I wish I could not see you," used to say the boys who always managed to get the thinnest slice, looking through it.

Like all boys they used to fight often but, by necessity, they also used to help each other and tried as much as they could not to be a burden to mother.

The poor mother!... she had quite a time of it. Wash this and wash that; patch this and re-patch that; the younger ones dirtying all over the place. She indeed had a hard time.

And where did all of them sleep? Well; the girls with mother, the boys on the floor on straw bags and father... (too late, poor man) on an old settee full of broken springs, beside his work bench.

Notwithstanding all this, they grew quite healthy.

Romualdo was one of the youngest and smallest of the boys. He was quite skinny, with a pale square face and two deep set eyes under thick eyebrows. He had thin brown hair and long sideburns which framed a deceptively sad face. But he was a happy go lucky boy and in good health.

In good health he was when an Italian chap who had made a fortune in Scotland, so they said, offered him a job in his fish and chip shop there.

He was just about sixteen and went off with him to Glasgow to be a scullery boy; better than carrying those dammed baskets of rocks on his shoulders up a steep path to the construction yard of the new Dam.

They said that the first Italians to go to this Country called Scotland had made fortunes. It was actually in the kind of job none of the locals liked to do: frying fish and chips until midnight and longer, in front of a coal fire that churned your stomach.

As soon as they got back from Italy they put him to work. He started every morning draining the oil from the enormous frying pan, as big as the bell of Barga, and cleaning it. Then he took the ashes out of the spent fire, polished the bench seats, washed the front step and polished it with Cardinal Red, very important to show zeal in general cleanliness, then, by machine, he peeled two bags of potatoes, at the weekend three or four. After which, at precisely one o'clock, he would go to the boss's house for lunch, usually a large plate of spaghetti, a glass of wine and some fruit. At night they always had fish and chips in the shop.

They really treated him like one of the family and he repaid them with conscientious work and loyalty.

In the afternoon, together with the boss, they went back to the shop to fillet the fish and at night, to start with, his work consisted mainly in stocking the fire with large lumps of coal, just like on a locomotive. But, after a year or so, having learnt the necessary English, he was allowed to serve at the counter. The pay was quite good, two pounds per week of which half was sent to his parents in Italy.

He continued working like this for another five years and when an old Italian from another town died Romualdo used his savings and a loan to buy his own fish and chip shop.

His kind and gentle nature endeared him to the locals and his business prospered well. He modernised the shop and installed cast iron friers while he too, was now employing a boy and a shop assistant. He felt justly proud.

Ten years after he left Italy he returned to his native village on holiday. A proper gentleman he looked like in his grey suit and hat, a gold chain in his waistcoat pocket and spats on his black and white shoes.

His only brother and sister still in the village, nephews and nieces, welcomed him with great emotion and put on a huge party for him. His father, now a frail and short sighted man was extremely emotional and his mother cried with joy.

He brought with him a nice little fortune: his brother had taken over the village bakery and needed new machinery, a nephew needed a chainsaw, someone else a sewing machine and others medicine or to replace a lame mule. He could not refuse. So he made them all happy and when he left Italy for Scotland, some months later, he was quite penniless.

This went on for several years until well, just imagine! At the age of almost forty he took a wife. His sister from Aberdeen who had emigrated there and married a fellow Italian years earlier, came to the wedding with her family.

The bride to be was a woman of Irish origins, as was the priest who would marry them.

"She's a Catholic and a religious woman," he said, congratulating Romualdo's sister.

"I'm happy that at least he's marrying a Catholic," she told him, wiping away a tear.

The wedding ceremony in the chapel was beautiful and very moving... but... poor chap... he looked so pitiful beside the woman. She was a good eight inches taller than he was and with a strong bone structure. She was blonde, perhaps ten years younger than he was and seemed not to have cheekbones, which made her chin large and rounded. Her eyes were small and deep-set, with no eyelashes and the merest hint of eyebrows. She was not altogether ugly in the true sense of the word and she had a certain charm and a deal of selfassurance which expressed itself in pride and character.

Where he'd fished her from? no one knew!

The following year they went to Italy.

His generosity soon became restrained: a few lire here and there, on the quiet, until she became aware of it, that is.

"It's very undignified," she used to say. "Just like handing out charity."

Immediately she took a dislike to the village, with all those women dressed in black and full of what she called servility as they would not even allow her to lift a chair! And the children... always intensely curious, staring at her and embarrassing her. Then there was the small matter of hygiene. The toilet was outside in the back garden and the kids used to spy on her when she went there.

Romualdo sprang to the defence of his native village. "It's exactly the same in Scotland," he said, "just look at the tenements with their communal toilets – and there are the back-garden privies, just like these here. In Ireland, it's even worse!"

She resented his taking sides with the village. "I am not Irish; I was born in Scotland, I'm a Scot and what's more I'm proud of it!" she shouted.

When it came to pride, she displayed perhaps more of it than the occasion warranted. She became aloof and withdrawn and decided to return home as soon as possible.

Romualdo did not object and consented with little reluctance.

It was the way she spoke to him and the tone of her voice which soon convinced him there was no point in arguing. Slowly but surely he was being led into blissful submission.

Everything else apart, he was then a happy man. She had a great capacity for work; she kept the house clinically clean, his working clothes were always spotlessly white and she was also a good cook. She soon realised, however, that the house was not big enough to occupy her mind fully so, a few months after their return home from Italy, she decided to sack the shop-assistant partly because she was becoming overly familiar with her husband, and assumed full control of the counter and the cash desk.

Their first son was born a year or so after their return from Italy. They named him Duncan, after one of the Kings of Scotland. Romualdo insisted their second son, born two years later, be called

Frederico after his father. In typical Scottish style, however, this was soon shortened to Fred. Needless to say, the birth of the two children put an abrupt end to further holidays in Italy.

The boys were growing up healthy and strong, so, their mother had less to keep her occupied and consequently she engaged a new assistant for the shop and would never allow the boys to go in there.

"It's a humiliating trade," she often said.

However humiliating the trade, it had provided her with the comforts of life; a new larger house, better furniture and carpets on the floor. All this, however, meant that Romualdo had to change his suit and shoes in the lobby when he went home for lunch, or late at night after he finished frying which was at about eleven o'clock when she would drop in to reset the cash register and collect the day's takings. On Saturdays she paid the assistant and before closing always made sure the door was locked properly.

"He's not much good at those sorts of things, he is good at frying, though. After all, that's why we have such a good business."

As things went, he was not particularly bothered and tended just to accept her little ways. What else could he do? There were never any arguments; a clean shirt every morning; breakfast and lunch always ready on time, the kids well cared for and he had no worries. He had plenty of pocket money on his day off – Wednesday when, having donned his black shirt he went off to the Italian Club with his Fascist friends. It wasn't that he knew or cared what all this Fascist business was about, he simply identified it with his country, the country of his birth. It was for the company and for a game of cards as they used to do in his home village in Tuscany.

Sometimes they would meet in the basement of an Italian grocery in the Cowcaddens to chat over a glass of wine; what else could a man want?

His only sadness, actually, was the kids. Except for a week or two at some Scottish seaside resort in the summer, he hardly ever saw them. In the morning, when he left for the fish market they were still in bed; at lunch time they were at school and by the time he got home again at night they were back in bed. As if this was not enough, they seemed to have been avoiding him for some time now even to the point of turning their heads away when he tried to give then a goodnight kiss.

It all stemmed from that contemptuous school insult, "Dirty Itai", even though they were the cleanest boys of the class. Their mother, of course, was furious: "You tell them that your mother is a Scot and proud of it!" she said. She also went to the school headmaster to complain. Romualdo slowly found himself increasingly isolated and ignored; if not despised.

To make things worse, the Abyssinian War came along with its ant-Fascist and anti-Mussolini propaganda which systematically found its way into the boys' bloodstream. To spite their father they stuck a poster of Mussolini on a board and used it as a target for darts practice. "It's only a game," the mother used to say, while Romualdo tried hard to look unconcerned.

To avoid any further adverse influence on their education, she sent them to a private school. However, after a year and a great waste of money, the headmaster of the school sent them back home saying they were troublesome, pig headed and lazy.

She refused to give in, so she sent them to music classes instead. There they seemed to do much better and, within a year or two, the house filled with all types of musical instruments: saxophones, clarinets, violins, a piano and even a drum kit which drew strong protests from the neighbours.

In the meantime, Romualdo kept on frying and yet more frying. The poor man felt so intimidated and sick of his life at home that, had he been able to, or had he still not loved his family, he would have avoided going home altogether. In an effort to console himself he turned to write letter after letter to his sister in Italy saying and pretend that everything was wonderful. During World War II he continued sending the letters through the Red Cross.

By the end of the war he was in failing health and was well over sixty years old. He longed to see his native village in Italy just one last time before he died, but no one would go with him. His sons preferred to go their own way and, in any case, they had never bothered to learn the language and Nancy, his wife, was not at all keen on travelling. He therefore resigned himself to never seeing his beloved village again and he died a few years later at the age of sixty-six.

The funeral was an important occasion; after all, everything had to be done property considering the number of friends and relations from the North of Scotland who would be there. The Funeral Mass was conducted by the old priest who had married him, and by Don Cruzzillo, the Xavieran Father of the Italian Mission to Scotland.

His passing was sadly mourned by everyone who knew him both within and outside the Italian Community.

*

Twenty years or more had passed since the news of Romualdo's death was taken to the village. His old sister passed away a few months later, but in a small village, sitting outside the houses in the cool of the evenings or conversing in the cafés, people went on reminiscing. Romualdo was well remembered back home because on his holidays he had always looked different; his spatters and his gold watch chain. Villagers don't easily forget these things. Some will laugh and scorn; others will admire or envy. But they will talk and talk about it again and again for years.

There was by now great prosperity in the village; things had changed greatly since the departure of Romualdo in 1883; young people went on honeymoon to distant lands, no longer to slave and enrich other countries. So it happened that a grandson of Romualdo's sister got married and spent his honeymoon with a cousin in Glasgow. The couple travelled, visiting all the tourist main attractions: Edinburgh, Aberdeen, the Trossachs, Loch Lomond and finally, remembering Granny's tales of her good looking and generous brother who had lived and died in Scotland, decided to make some enquiries. They were lucky to find an old Italian gentleman who had known Romualdo and also knew the cemetery in which he had been buried.

They decided to go there and pay their respects. The old gentleman went with them.

Although much younger than Romualdo at the time they knew each other, they were quite friendly, said the old man; they used to play cards together and nearly every morning, after their purchases at the fish market, they met, with other Italians, for coffee at Coopers, in Saint Enoch's Square.

"He was a very quiet and gentle man," he said. "He did not look as if he was happy, though, particularly during the war. He was, perhaps, gently overpowered by his wife. A very strong woman. But he never stopped praising her. He had two handsome sons you know, God knows where they are now." The old man continued, "You see, the mother was Scots so they had nothing Italian except their blood," the old man paused a little, "I met her a few times; she was very kind, clever and a great worker Romualdo used to say. I have been told that she is still alive in a rest home for gentlewoman; very expensive places! She must be quite an age herself."

They had been walking for some time along the avenues of the cemetery, stopping at intervals to read the names of numerous Italians buried there, this being the only Catholic cemetery in town, down the London Road. Many beautiful monuments imported from Italy had been vandalised; there was disorder and neglect all around. Vandals, seemingly, raid the place quite often, knocking down crosses and namestones. Some Angels and Madonnas lay damaged on the ground.

At last they reached the area where, the old gentleman remembered, they had buried poor Romualdo. The place was like a jungle. Weeds and bracken grew as tall as some of the old stones still standing. The avenues were scarred by recurring rains.

They searched here and there but to no avail.

"It was here," confirmed the old man. "It has got to be here!... " Pausing thoughtfully for a while he added, "Well, I may be wrong. It was so long ago."

They decided to go back to the cemetery office where the small obese man, having turned page after page of a large book, confirmed what he had already told them showing great displeasure "Of course it's there! Just where I told you."

"But we have looked all over."

"Go and look again; it's there I am telling you."

They all went back looking at every gravestone but again found nothing.

The man who, by the way he was dressed in black suit with a very tight jacket and a bowler hat – was thought to be the Director of the cemetery, on seeing them coming back a second time evidently disillusioned, was quite furious. He got up from his chair without a word said and, having picked up a measuring tape from a shelf, mumbling God knows what, pushed his way out of the office and briskly started walking towards the areas where he was sure old Romualdo lay.

The visitors could hardly keep up with him.

When he got to the spot uttering in disdain the numbers, he started measuring and checking a map he had taken with him. "Fifteen meters from the wall... eight from this corner... twenty from the Northern Avenue... " and suddenly pushing aside the weeds, he shouted: "... here it is! I told you... he has no gravestone; only a number!" and, having re-coiled his measuring tape, left hastily in anger.

In the spot indicated, the little man had implanted a large bolt with a metal number on it.

"Looks like the number of his house off the Dumbarton Road," said the old man.

Mercifully, on the same spot, surrounded by a jungle of weeds and bracken, a wild thistle grew and, at the very base of that rusty bolt, in defiance of that sacrilege, covered in sparkling dew drops, a little white daisy gleamed, fragile and gentle, like snow.

The Rotten Apple

It did not take much convincing!

He had been nursing the idea for over thirty years; agonised and tormented by a feeling of guilt he could not suppress.

In his mind everything still looked so vivid; the green fields, the patchy heather against the hill, the people, the war, the Prisoner of war camp, the merciless rain and the feeble sound of bagpipes in the distance when a farmer next to the farm he was billeted on kept practising for hours.

Scotland!...

For him it was more than the name of a country; it had become a magnet, a force he had been resisting for far too long, yearning and hoping.

So it did not take much to convince him, since he was now retired and the land given to him by the Government when it was expropriated from a rich landlord who was only using it for hunting and other pleasurable pursuits, had now become a joy to look at; flourishing with fruit, olive trees and vine that yielded some of the best wine in the area. His two sons were indeed capable of looking after it, hinting and often stressing that they could indeed do well without him. He finally agreed; he would go! He feigned resentment! "You are wanting to get rid of me," he said, but he was so excited that for nights and nights before the fateful departure he found it quite impossible to sleep.

They were not wanting to get rid of him; they were hoping he would relax and take life easy, now that he had retired. "Maybe on his return, one way or another, he may find peace."

His friends at the café would tease him, "What are you doing now that you are retired?" and he would answer, "Just playing about! Little light work such as pruning the vine, decanting and bottling wine and oil." But they just could not keep him away from the orchard! Quite often he was found tackling the hardest chores.

His elder son was married and had two handsome boys of seven and three. He was now in charge of the orchard; he was a good son.

The old man loved his grandsons very much and spent a lot of time with them walking or taking the older one to school. He insisted upon the whole family being at the airport to say goodbye.

He still remembered some English he had learned in the POW camps and he would find no difficulties getting to Scotland.

One fine crispy morning they all boarded the shooting brake and left for Naples airport, about forty minutes away. Dawn was just breaking in the East and a thick mist lingered at the summit of mount Vesuvius. At first they were all joking and laughing but as they neared the airport the traffic grew heavier they fell silent. He suddenly became sad and thoughtful. He was assailed by doubts and asked himself if he was not a fool, but there was no way back.

The goodbyes in the lounge of the airport were quite subdued; he hardly uttered a word while the rest tried to cheer him up.

He boarded the plane for his two and a half hour flight to London. The sun cast a splendor of light on the bay and the city; mount Vesuvius and the green hills beyond. He glimpsed the scene from the plane and his heart trembled with emotion.

He had a good flight enjoying the company of another countryman.

From the airport he took a Taxi to Euston station just in time for an early train to Glasgow.

In Glasgow he found a small hotel in the city centre near the railway station, and after a light meal in a Pizza Parlour he returned to his hotel room.

It was almost eight and too early to go to bed.

The sun, setting low in the burning sky, shone through the curtains of a wide bay window revealing a glorious sunset, but he was not in the mood for such things and fully dressed he slumped on the bed, staring at the low ceiling while his mind wandered back to the squalor of the military prison were he spent the most miserable time of his life. From the street below came the constant hubbub of city traffic and he slowly started remembering and reminiscing, beginning from the night on which he and his companion had been taken from the farm they had been billeted; a fateful night imprinted in his memory as with a chisel.

He and his friend had just returned from a hard day at work in the fields, they had just had a quick meal and were preparing themselves to go out for a walk. Roberto was setting things ready to write a letter home on the way back and Giuseppe was just about to finish with his turn at washing up. In the East darkness was fast progressing and the full moon amid shimmering stars, seemed to admire the straight freshly cut furrows, fruit of their labour, while in the West night was about to swallow the last rosy rays of the autumn sun.

On the muddy track sloping down to the main road, four beams of moving light flickered along the dry stone wall and the winding privet edge that lined it, while the strident noise of a siren angrily shattered the silence of the moonlit valley.

The two vehicles came to a halt in the yard in front of the big farmhouse and a number of soldiers, rifles at the ready, hurriedly spread in all directions. Two police officers dismounted from a car with a red light on its roof and moved decisively towards the farmer, waiting quite puzzled, on the steps of the farmhouse.

From their billets, some sixty yards away, beyond the sheds, the two Italian POWs craned their necks through the blackened attic window trying to see what was happening, each with fear in his heart; both doing their best to look unconcerned. Trembling, they had returned to their chores, when the small door from the narrow staircase suddenly opened and the two policemen, followed by Mr McPhail, the farmer, and the two military policemen burst in. One of these, a sergeant, ordered them to collect their personal things while Mr McPhail continued to demand explanations and the reason why the prisoners were being taken away just when they were much needed on the farm.

The police knew nothing or pretended to know nothing.

The two prisoners were unceremoniously led to a tarpaulin covered lorry which, followed by the Police car, returned at speed the same way they had come; darting through the darkness of a star studded sky while the moon itself suddenly appearing dim and sad hid behind thin fleeting clouds.

An Italian Warrant Officer, who acted as a liaison with the British Command and was in effect the Italian Commandant of the camp, was informed of the arrests and told that the two miscreants were Roberto Calvante from Ancona and Giuseppe Calcaterra from Naples. He was not yet told of the presumed offenses and soon the whole camp was seething with conjectures and innuendo.

It was known that two policemen had been to see the British Commanding Officer early that afternoon and that they had returned later in company of a beautiful blond girl accompanied by what it was presumed to be her parents. The latter, by he way they dressed, were indubitably labourers or farm hands. The man wore a short brown jacket, riding breeches and a flat cap and the woman a red overcoat slightly shorter that a blue and white tartan skirt beneath. The girl had a beautiful face in which two big blue eyes shone like pearls. Thick blond hair hung in curls on either side of her face and neck.

The prisoners, some of whom had seen very few women over the last three to four years, thought she was very attractive and there were also some misconceived wolf whistles.

Roberto and Giuseppe spent the night huddled in their bunk beds in the restricted space of their cell both pretending to know nothing of what was afoot; each looked accusingly at the other, feigning innocence but in their hearts they dreaded what would come to light at daybreak. They were not in the mood to confide in each other as they hoped in the possibility of being accused of something other than what they feared it would be, but they could not sleep and in the uncertain silence of the night there were lots of sighs and prayers.

Assuming the worst, each was calculating the consequences of his indiscretions. It was, in any case, "a consensual affair" even if this was "forbidden fruit", as decency would have us call it. In an optimistic mood each foresaw a penalty of seven to ten days in jail and each on his own account was resigned to the maximum. What then if they were sentenced for something for which they were innocent?

It seemed unlikely but, in a climate of prejudice, nothing was impossible.

None too soon, reveille broke the thread of their thoughts. Night had been dragging and they both felt quite tired, yet, they still had to face a fateful day. It was only seven o'clock and still dark.

A British corporal of the guard, opened the cell door, handed them their personal things and showed them the toilets. Later they had breakfast: bread, butter, marmalade and coffee, brought from the camp kitchens. Nothing like the breakfast Mrs McPhail prepared at the farm, where every morning they had a farmer's feast consisting of two fried eggs with bacon, toasted bread and as much milk as you could drink, all together with her husband and the two boys.

The two POWs thought for a moment that they were about to be released, but this was not to be. With eloquent signs, the corporal told them "No," although they were free to move around the small courtyard outside the cells.

From this sort of courtyard in front of the prison, they could see the British Commandant's office, in the vicinity of which they noticed some unusual activity. Among the many policemen and officials who were moving this way and that, they spotted Mr and Mrs McPhail to whom they waved smilingly while the corporal was taking them back to the room where they had had breakfast.

They waited for a few minutes in fearful silence. Soon afterwards an army officer, a lieutenant, entered the room. In perfect Italian he said that his name was Lieutenant Wolfson and that, in their own best interests, they should listen carefully to what he had to say.

The three of them sat down around a table and having laid on it the briefcase he was carrying, Lieutenant Wolfson began by saying:

"I have been assigned as your lawyer."

One of the two began to ask a question, but the lieutenant silenced him by putting his finger to his lips.

"Please listen it me. I have something to say and even if it offends you, keep quiet. It is a fact that you Italians easily reveal your guilt even as you deny it. Therefore you are at the mercy of an unforgiving investigator. He will have no doubts about your guilt. With threats and inducements he will talk you into confessing. Although I am a lieutenant in the British Army, my job, on orders of my superiors, is to defend you to the best of my ability, whether you are guilty or not. In civilian life I was a barrister by profession and I do not like to lose. However, I do need your full co-operation. First of all, I wish to advise you that military Law, likewise the civil Law in this country, requires the prosecution to prove guilt, while the accused has the right to defend himself by denying the crime and even refusing to speak or answer any questions that may incriminate him. I am not sure yet whether or not this will come to trial. But if a trial does take place, the accused cannot be questioned if he has not first been called to testify by his defence barrister. At that time he must tell the truth or be guilty of perjury. I repeat, I do not know yet what the charges are, but I know that they will shortly begin questioning you. Before the interrogations start, you have the right to have a lawyer. I do not know what this is all about and I do not want to find out from you, even if you should so wish. My advice for the moment is to deny everything, and keep on denying it whether or not it is true. I hope you will not let me down. Now I will go and seek information. There is no need to get up.

Lieutenant Wolfson picked up his briefcase and went out.

The two men sat looking at one another and, a few minutes later, they were led back to their cells. Once there, they began to risk a few satisfied comments about Lieutenant Wolfson and how well he spoke Italian.

Immediately afterwards, as the Lieutenant had warned them, the interrogations began. Roberto Torquato was the first to be called back into the same small room in the prison.

The interrogator, obviously a policeman, was dressed in civilian clothes and revealed himself to be very kind or so it seemed. He was a middle-aged man in his forties with black hair and a smiling face. He began by offering Roberto a cigarette, but he refused.

Then, through an interpreter, a woman aged about fifty, he asked him from which city he came from.

"From Rome?" Roberto answered.

"The detective says that he has been to Venice, Verona and Lake Garda. After the war he wants to visit Rome, Florence and Naples," the woman translated.

"Very Good!" said the prisoner "Beautiful places!"

The conversation then continued something like this:

"Do you have a wife back home in Italy?"

"No."

"Are your parents still alive; your brothers and sisters?"

"Yes."

The detective paused a while, then, looking straight into Roberto eyes:

"I am sorry," he said, "you are in very hot water. An intelligent chap like you should at least have taken proper precautions and not made her pregnant."

Avoiding the trap, Roberto said:

"What?... Who?... What are you talking about?"

"You know very well, who! Look, you should know that the Court will show mercy in cases where the accused immediately admits his guilt and instead of a sentence of say, five years, which is the maximum in such cases, you could get away with a year or less. It is in your interests not to waste our time, for we have all the proof we need and, if you insist on denying the charges there will be no alternative but five years in prison."

"I do not know anything," Roberto said, trying to remain calm and not to show concern.

"What I am really trying to find out," the detective continued, "is whether there are any extenuating circumstances. If you wanted to help yourself, for example, you could tell the Court that she had provoked you; that she had incited and encouraged you. You could also say that it had all been the girl's fault, which would be to your advantage."

"I don't know what are you talking about." Roberto shouted.

"Oh come on!" the detective insisted, showing some impatience, "you know very well that Italian prisoners of war are forbidden from fraternising with British girls. With all the proof we have, you cannot deny it; it will only make things worse. If you do; I really can't help you," he said. The detective feigning sadness and pretending to leaf through his folder and pretending to seek help, suddenly sprang the question: "What was the girl's name?"

Roberto had been on the point of telling! But he quickly collected his wits and said with some force:

"I know nothing! Nothing, you understand?"

The detective continued with this line of questioning for a further ten minutes. Then he called Giuseppe, to whom he repeated the same arguments, using all the usual tricks. However, he too admitted nothing, sticking to the lawyer's advice.

The same morning both of them were taken to see the camp commandant, who told them in no uncertain terms that he was very annoyed. The Italian Warrant Officer and Lieutenant Wolfson were also in the office.

"I have been told," the camp commandant said after showing his severe disappointment, "that the guilty party has decided not to confess. That person ought to know that he is damaging his innocent companion because one of you, the innocent one, could go back to the farm immediately. In fact, Mr McPhail will return here in a while, so if the guilty party will step forward now, I will do all I can to help him."

No one moved.

The commandant made a signal to a guard and first the detective, then another policeman and finally the girl and the woman, who was supposed to be her mother entered the office.

The girl was smiling as though this was all great fun, and she immediately began waving at the two prisoners who had been lined up against the wall.

The scene that followed was a revelation and caused general bewilderment. The girl was invited to point out who had seduced her. Still smiling; a sort of vacant smile, she almost literally threw herself at Roberto, who was standing at the left side.

"Good," said the detective satisfied, noticing the boy's great consternation. He then turned to the girl and took her by the arm. But, she pulled herself away with a jerk, freeing herself, and looking terribly cross. The girl began to smile again and took Giuseppe's hand, "Hello" she murmured, sweetly.

It is quite impossible to describe the general bewilderment. The boys, like all others, appeared absolutely lost.

After a few moments hesitation, the girl was hustled almost forcibly from the office, all the while smiling and waving at the prisoners. A few minutes later they, too, were taken to their cells.

Although the situation was still worrying, the plot thickened with the revelation that they seemed to have a joint mistress, which was unbelievably odd. They looked daggers at each other but when they finally got back to their cells, forgetting the predicament they found themselves in, they began to laugh and throw questions at each other.

"Both of us?... Is that possible?... you dirty cad."

"I would never have believed such a thing."

"Me neither!... Will it be bad for us?"

"Let us hope not. Just remember what Lieutenant Wolfson said."

"So how did you come to meet her?" Giuseppe asked Roberto.

"I believe you know all about it yourself, it must have been in the same way as you. I was making my way to the dam at the top of the hill when I saw her standing on a small path near the undergrowth. It was already getting dark. Smiling, she called to me. When I moved to go towards her, she began to run. I was undecided, so I stopped. She stopped too and, still smiling, she continued to wave and call to me but when I moved, she ran away in fear, it seemed. If I ran to catch up with her she would run all the harder. Soon we came to a yard completely enclosed by a dry stone wall and with many little huts in it, from which came the cackling of chickens and the grunting of pigs. I hid for fear that there were people about. Then I heard a woman calling: 'Mary... Mary... is that you?' She went into a cottage and came out a little later with a bucket which could have contained pig-feed. Darkness had already fallen. By the light coming from a window, I saw her immediately running towards me behind a bush. She took me by the hand and led me into an empty hut. What else could I do? No more than ten minutes later we got dressed again. She pressed a note into my hand and ran off towards the house. The note said... "

"I know what the note said." Mine said, "Wednesday, next week," interrupted Giuseppe.

"Mine... Was Monday."

Even if it had gone on this way for about four months no one ever guessed that she was a mentally retarded girl. She never talked and none of them had seen her in any other circumstances, everyone kept the secret for fear that something would happen to spoil such a convenient arrangement.

"And now?"

They looked at each other dumbstruck.

In the camp commandant's office the Italian Warrant Officer and the chaplain, Father Puzillo, were arguing in favour of the prisoners while the British police stood around perplexed re-appraising the situation. The camp commandant asked the detective if he had known about the girl's mental disability.

"No," he replied. "The report was made by her step-parents and it seemed right, in the first instance, to make some preliminary enquiries."

"What about you, Lieutenant Wolfson?"

"Until this morning, sir, I did not even know what this was all about."

The camp commandant, a colonel, was an elderly man of relatively small stature. He had white hair which was still thick, and a kind, pink face. He spoke slowly, as though weighing every word. He was a courteous and patient man.

"So, what do you propose," he said, sitting down with his arms crossed on his chest, looking straight into the eyes of the detective.

"I must stress that the girl is pregnant," said the detective, and it seems as though both prisoners have committed the crime of fraternisation."

"It seems to me," added Lieutenant Wolfson, "that it will be impossible to sustain the charges. The girl is undoubtedly mentally handicapped and does not have the slightest notion of right or wrong. Being retarded as she is, it cannot be excluded that she has frequently been a sex victim, and consequently, used to sexual abuse for years. If my judgement, based on what I have seen and heard, is confirmed by a psychiatrist, her promiscuity could induce her to do this with any man she finds sexually attractive. In this office, for example, she approached the two men who are much younger than us and who both seem to have the undeniable Latin attraction."

"We will have to see whether she behaves in a similar way when asked to identify other prisoners," the detective interjected.

"You should very well know that such a subterfuge cannot be admitted as evidence, but, why resort to tricks? The girl's mental condition would suggest that her reactions are somewhat unpredictable like when you tried to move her away from the first prisoner. She is subject to sudden changes of mood, passive and acquiescent one minute, active and violent the next. It would seem to me sir, that it would be in the interests of the girl, who would be spared unnecessary suffering, if we effect the release of the prisoners I have been assigned to defend and return them to the farm where they can usefully help with the country's need for food. To proceed further would be a waste of time."

"Before doing that, Sir," interrupted the Detective taking his leave, "please wait till I have consulted my Chief Inspector."

Meanwhile back in the prison the prisoners had supper and were visited by Mr McPhail who brought them some apples and one of Mrs McPhail's pies. Then came the Italian Warrant Officer to tell them how things had gone and what had happened. He also told them that Lieutenant Wolfson had been born in Milan of Jewish-Italian parents who had lived there for generations. They had fled to Britain in 1937 to escape Fascist persecution.

Since he had been born and brought up in Milan, it was clear to them now why he spoke Italian so well, but they could not understand why he had fled Italy. Why?... What persecution?"

On taking his leave, the Warrant Officer reminded them what Lieutenant Wolfson had advised: namely to admit nothing.

In due course the detective consulted a gynaecologist who, having visited the girl and confirmed that she was three months pregnant, announced that he would be able to take blood quite safely from the unborn baby to determine his paternity.

The prisoners were taken to the infirmary where a blood sample was taken from their little fingers.

No news was forthcoming. The time passed quite uneventfully. Mrs McPhail came nearly every day or so with baskets of fruit and the usual apple pie. When it came to it, the prison was nothing more than confinement. They were regularly taken under escort for long walks in the country, past fields freshly ploughed and others lush with grass on which cows and sheep peacefully grazed.

One rainy morning they had just finished breakfast when a sergeant of the guard appeared and told Giuseppe to follow him. Trembling and with his heart in his mouth, the poor fellow walked the hundred metres which separated the prison from the Commandant's office.

The commandant's office was full of policemen and detectives in civilian clothes. Lieutenant Wolfson waved at him to reassure him, while a detective, probably an inspector, read the charge and informed him of his rights through the interpreter.

"... that you, POW Giuseppe Calcaterra fraternised with a British woman and did enter into a sexual relationship with her, taking advantage of her mental condition and making her pregnant. Do you have anything to say?"

"No. It cannot be true!" shouted Giuseppe pale with emotion and fear.

Lieutenant Wolfson looked at him, telling him silently to keep quiet but, protesting his innocence, he was led away by two MP's to a lorry which then sped off.

Roberto was freed, and returned to the farm where Mr McPhail was delighted to see him back at work, although he felt sorry for poor Giuseppe.

The military prison situated in the moors some fifty kilometres from the camp, was a group of wooden buildings encircled by double fence. It was a barren, marshy place where grass, accumulated over the millennia, had decayed to form a layer of peat about fifty centimetres deep, which, cut and dried, was used in fires instead of logs.

Most of the prisoners were either Italians or Germans, but there were also a few Poles, Austrians and Hungarians. There were one hundred prisoners in all, employed to extract the peat, which was particularly arduous work due to the icy winds that were a feature of the area.

About ten days after he arrived at the prison, Giuseppe had a visit from Lieutenant Wolfson. He started by saying that it was impossible to refute the proof of paternity, but added that he was counting on extenuating circumstances for a minimum sentence or even freedom. So he wanted to be told the whole story of how Giuseppe had met the girl, and to be fully satisfied that he had a valid defence to present although, in a climate of prejudice, it paid to be cautious and not have too many illusions.

The trial took place in the prison canteen and proved to be a brief affair. It was all over in less than half an hour, covering almost exclusively arguments for the defence, at which Lieutenant Wolfson excelled. Based on the facts already given to the detective in the Camp Commandant's office and on Calcaterra's account of the circumstances in which he had met the girl, which showed the accused to be the victim of an ingenious seduction, there seemed to be no case against the accused.

Calcaterra stood in the middle of the room, flanked by two burly soldiers in their impeccable uniforms with white belts and red caps, and looked intently at the three officers behind a plain table. They were the judges in this court martial and they remained impassive to the clever speeches by Lieutenant Wolfson, betraying nothing of what they thought while retiring to consider the case.

The Colonel, the Italian Warrant Officer, the Chaplain and several other policemen were talking in a satisfied manner, some trying to cheer him up and give him something to hope for.

Lieutenant Wolfson had concluded his address by asking for the prisoner's release, and there was an air of guarded optimism. The three judges returned. The presiding judge having signalled his readiness, everyone stood up for the verdict to be delivered.

In the introduction the presiding judge speaking for the Court, noted that, although they appreciated the line taken by the defence, the human circumstances of the case and the fact that Italy had already signed an armistice with Britain, the statute on prisoners of war remained in force until the day of repatriation. It was therefore impossible to release the Italian prisoner, Giuseppe Calcaterra, from the penal provisions of the International Convention on the right of nations detaining prisoners to apply a prohibition on fraternisation with the relevant penalties for breach of the convention:

"Taking into account the extenuating circumstances, of which the Court takes due cognisance, the Court sentences the prisoner, Giuseppe Calcaterra to the minimum penalty prescribed by law: nine months imprisonment in an open military prison with full remission as allowed by law."

Swallowing back his tears, Calcaterra remained impassive and when the three judges rose to leave he bowed to them in thanks.

The open prison, Lieutenant Wolfson said, was a detention camp more or less like the prison where he had already spent a month, therefore there were only eight months of his sentence left. With one or two months of remission he could be out in June or July of 1946 and, since the repatriation programme was in full swing, he would undoubtedly be repatriated before then.

Giuseppe thanked him warmly, leaving in the company of two soldiers from the barracks he waved to the others who were there.

The open prison was the one where he had already spent some time awaiting trial; it was open to all the winds and storms. On days when it was dry the prisoners worked at cutting the peat, while on wet days Giuseppe studied to learn a bit of English or learnt to play the guitar that a Polish soldier had brought with him. To his great joy,

the McPhails from the farm came to visit him one Sunday every month, bringing with them one of Mrs McPhail's famous apple pies.
In a short time he learnt to play the guitar and soon became a favourite in the camp with his Neapolitan songs, some of which were sad and melancholy like "Core e Mamma",

> Dico... Ma'
> Sa che buo'fa?
> Fa nu vuto ca me passasse,
> Stá nustalgia
>
> (I say, Mother,
> Know what to do!
> Pray for my
> Nostalgia to leave me...)

and other songs like "Canzone Appassionata", "Munasterio e Santa Chiara" and "Nun tengo cchiù lacrime!"

A bout of sadness overtook him when he was told that the prison camp he had been in had been closed and all the prisoners repatriated. Then he found out that the girl had been sterilised and shut away in a hospital for handicapped children after giving birth to a healthy, brown-haired boy. He was deeply touched but said nothing. McPhail told him the boy had been put into care by the Social Services.

Finally, his sentence was reviewed and reduced by two months but he had to wait a further month before he was put on a ship direct to Naples.

*

The relative silence in the city street below made him aware he had spent almost five hours in his hotel room reliving those far-off days: he looked at the clock, it was almost midnight. He thought of the McPhails who would be waiting for him the following morning and he imagined them as he had left them: he steadfast and severe, but in reality honest and kind, and she pleasant and attentive, always bustling about and smiling to herself. How they would marvel at seeing him now, old and decayed, with a wrinkled and serious face.

He could hardly wait to see again the people he called the best friends he had ever had in his life. He had never forgotten them and every Christmas he had sent them a card.

Early the next morning he took the train and left on his three hour journey to Perthshire, thinking of all sorts of surprises that might await him concerning the child he had never known. He arrived at the railway station in the late morning. The McPhail's were there to meet him, but at first they did not recognise him, nor he them.

Mr McPhail was now aged over seventy and his wife was only a few years younger. He was still fit and hard-working, had white hair as was to be expected and he wore a Harris tweed jacket with a shirt, tie and polished shoes, something rarely seen on him at the farm. She wore a beaver coat. Altogether, they looked like two proper gentlepeople. When he recognised them, Giuseppe felt a bit embarrassed and awkward, but they ran towards him and embraced him warmly. They were all soon talking as though they had only parted a few days ago.

Once in the car, they took him to the farm, which was now run by his sons, and proudly showed him the new milking machine, the newly equipped cowsheds and the new hen-house for raising battery chickens. Giuseppe remarked that his own property was now also a proper orchard with oranges, mandarins and grapes which made exceptionally good wine. Finally they went into the house and the conversation turned to the subject of the little Italian boy abandoned by fate.

"We have not heard a word of him for many years past," said Mrs McPhail. "You know, the girl was taken into hospital and the baby was put into care. The girl's foster parents, who were workers on Lord Mansfield's estate which adjoins this one, left after a few years to work at tree planting up in the Highlands. We mentioned the case to a few friends but they were all very sceptical. Tomorrow though, we will go out and hope that we can find out what happened."

When he awoke the next morning the sun was still low in the sky, bathing his room in a pale, rosy glow. It was six o'clock and the farm buildings were already a hive of activity. He did not want to wait until he was called to breakfast. He got up and went to watch the family and the farm workers milking the cows, sterilising the milk and making butter, piling up the hay and cleaning the hen-house, until everyone came into the farmhouse for breakfast.

As in times past, there was ham and fried eggs in abundance, with toast and large glasses of milk. When breakfast was over he went with Mr McPhail to visit the neighbouring estate of Lord Mansfield.

The great mansion, in the Adam's style, was situated imposingly at the end of a long, tree-lined drive. In front of the house there was an ornamental fountain located in the centre of a finely cut lawn. They were shown into the Factor's office and he seemed surprised by the information they asked for:

"An employee who worked on the estate twenty years ago? The file must surely have been destroyed by now. They lived in a tied cottage, you say? So many people lived in these cottages over the years!"

They made their apologies and left for the village about three miles away. On their arrival, they went to the Registry Office where a kind girl was happy to be able to help them:

"What was the child called?"

"We do not know."

"So how can I help you, then?"

"We know that he was born in June, 1946. His father was unknown."

"Oh... Well, let us see." She went and fetched the register for June, 1946.

"June? Do you know what date?"

"No. It was somewhere around mid-June, I think."

"June... June... no father... that is, I mean father unknown."

After looking through the three pages that covered June 1946, she confirmed that none of the babies in that month had been illegitimate.

"But tell me, why do you want to know this?"

In a few words they explained the reason for their search and that the new-born infant had been immediately placed in the care of the Social Services.

"Ah," the girl exclaimed. "That changes everything completely! The traces of a possible search may be lost, sometimes the birth is registered in the area where the hospital is located. I suggest you try and get a list of local hospitals, although it seems unlikely that they will be able to divulge names, at least based on what you have told me."

"So?... You think we are wasting our time?"

"I do not want to raise false hopes; you may have a bit of luck. You just never know."

They thanked the lady and left trying to plan the next move. It seemed as though there was nothing else for it but to go back to the farm disappointed.

Over the next four or five days they took advice from lawyers, private detectives, the welfare and social authorities, but all of them said it was hopeless. The help given by Mr McPhail and the prolonged hospitality in his home, although given generously, began to make Giuseppe feel embarrassed. He had bought a tourist air fare and felt it would have been insensitive of him to accept a further week of hospitality while waiting for the date of his return flight. He had already thought about finding an excuse to leave and spend the few remaining days in Glasgow at an hotel, when a telephone call came from his eldest son in Italy who wanted to know how things had gone and whether there had been any results. Then he told Giuseppe that his two year-old grandson had caught scarlet fever.

There was no further need for excuses. He felt the call of his true family and of reality, from which he had been somewhat distant, being consumed by a paternal right that he did not really have. He felt sorry for himself and, as though suddenly he had seen the sunlight after an interminable time spent in darkness, he turned to announce his intention to return home.

He seemed to be a changed man. He was ready to forget a past that no longer made any sense; neither did he want to go and visit the old prison camp as he had planned to do. Anyway, it was probably a pile of old ruins.

He said goodbye to the McPhails and invited them to visit him at his home in Italy. Arriving in Glasgow, he bought a new airline ticket to Rome and out to Naples in order to depart as soon as possible. On the plane, though, he was unable to prevent himself from thinking again about the child with his own blood running in his veins. Where was he? Was he happy? At any rate, Giuseppe preferred to think he was. He would by now be nearly thirty.

Just then the image of that poor, unhappy girl sprang into his mind. He saw her face and the vacant smile that he had seen for the first time in daylight in the Camp Commandant's office. A trace of sadness clouded his face, which only a short time before, had been radiant with the joyous expectation of returning home.

The poor girl had been deprived of her child and locked away in an asylum because of her innocence and an overpowering natural instinct which had freed her from the precepts of so-called traditional values, but with cruel consequences. She had been put away to suppress and extinguish her primitive impulses with an almost casual gesture, the way one would snuff out a candle: she was a sinless soul, with a pure heart but no real awareness. She had been discarded and thrown away, just like a rotten apple. The thought almost made him cry.

The Bells of Don Comodo

In appearance he could have been just another schoolboy of seven or eight years of age. He was a shy boy, habitually reserved but inclined to be impetuous. He was ever ready to throw himself into the rough-and-tumble of occasionally dangerous games, and his calm and carefree exterior hid an inquisitive, astute mind and an almost obstinate will.

He was born and brought up in the shadow of the great bell tower which dominated the tangle of rustic houses stacked one on top of the other in his native village at the top of a hill straddling the rivers Bradano and Basento, in Lucania, a mountainous and poor region of Italy where he found himself unable to escape the harsh environmental apathy and boredom, which was made worse by the oppressive heat of some torrid afternoons. During the school summer holidays, when the peasants sweated in the harvest fields and the few left in the village were mercifully taking refuge in the pleasures of the siesta, he would retire to the north side of the church, in the shade, sitting on the cool steps, determined not to fall asleep. He was waiting perhaps, for the cool breeze of the evening when all his pals would be coming out for the usual games. But, if in appearances he was reduced to being part of the surrounding general immobility, his mind was restlessly probing the distant horizon, creating for himself a world of exciting adventures, infinitely greater than those of Pinocchio and more heroic than those of the Little Sardinian Drummer.

From his position he could follow the train from Taranto snaking its way for miles along the dry river bed, smoking and puffing until it disappeared within the stony bowels of the Tunnel under Calciano, the postal bus from Matera, noisily negotiating the road uphill towards the Capuchin Monastery and, in the evenings, the return home of the peasants along the dusty mule tracks.

Occasionally, filled with a strong desire to do something, he would stroll up and down the little square in front of the church, stop at an ants' nest to observe their labours, try to catch a creeping lizard or study the flight and flutter of ravens in and out of the ancient scaffold holes of the bell tower, but the bell tower was his major focus of attention and fascination. And the bells!

To ring the bells was his cherished ambition. He realised it was a silly ambition, but the imperative desire to do something new, anything to escape the boredom which nearly choked this spirit, would have been of relief and, above all, he would finally be able to silence that terrible sentence by Don Comodo every time he offered to ring the bells,

"No. You are too small. You cannot go up to ring the bells!"

The other, perhaps more compelling reason for wanting to climb the bell tower, whether or not to ring the bells, was the tale of wonderful views from there which he had heard from the older boys who were allowed up: distant mountains and villages up to Potenza itself on one side and, on the other, the great fertile green plains of Apulia, with a distant glimpse of the Adriatic Sea, just a thin blue line on the horizon.

Then, with a resigned shrug of his shoulders and an expectant smile of his face, he would retire to his preferred spot until the usual donkey came clip-clopping along carrying its load of straw below which its head and legs were barely visible, its ironshod hooves striking the paved road, to rouse him from his daydreams.

The solitary bell ringing Vespers and his pals already on the road would bring him back to reality. The sun was slowly disappearing behind the ragged ruins of the Capuchin Monastery; the gentle breeze brought a welcome coolness and, surrendering to the call of supper he would wend his way home with the almost irritating sound of the bell ringing in his ears.

*

Some several months later, on one of these foggy autumn days, the teacher of primary five, Miss Giuseppina, caught a nasty cold. Delighted, at the unexpected day off, the children were soon playing under the arches of the old monastery next door to the church. The monastery had at one time flourished and been home to a small group of Brothers of Charity, but it had since been converted into stables, stores and flats. Don Comodo lived in one of these flats, at the top of a wide, dark staircase.

He had the title of Archpriest and was a man of imposing stature who did not hide his reverent importance. He kept himself to himself and no one had ever seen him smiling. He hardly ever came out of his house except to go to church or mass or to lead a religious procession. However, due largely to the Sacristan who was also the village cobbler, he knew everything that went on in the village and since it must be said, not all the villagers were angels, he had many occasions to pour scorn and disdain on those of his parishioners who sinned, administering penances and indulgences from the Confessional in large quantities. On Sundays from the pulpit and even at solemn funeral masses, he would castigate those drunkards who beat their wives, those who quarrelled playing at cards and the boys who made eyes at the girls in the church. With monotonous regularly he admonished everyone on the dangers of fornication and immoral thoughts by which he himself, possibly, could have been afflicted.

Don Comodo loved his comforts and had no disdain for the good things in life. The Parish was quite rich in lands and houses and, it was said, the rents from these also paid for some of his nephews at the University in Naples.

Before the onset of winter Don Comodo made sure that he had enough wood for the fire and every Sunday, for three or four weeks in the autumn, his tenants would arrive with mules and donkeys unloading a large quantity of logs. He would interrupt the boys being taught their catechism, to get them to carry it upstairs by the armful, as though it were a game, and deposit it in large stacks along the corridor. Work completed, they would line up to receive a handful of dried figs and nuts.

Don Comodo, apparently, lived a quiet and peaceful life. Apart from living like a hermit (more or less), it was impossible to charge him with an indiscretion and thus he was able to remain uncensored, avoiding any malicious gossip. Rarely at masses would he pass round the collection plate. He avoided politics and hardly ever bothered or imposed himself on anybody; not even on the gentry at the hunting Club. He really kept himself to himself, and apart from his bad temper and his hatred of sinners, you could say that he was a good priest, always aware of his mission and the sanctity of his duties.

However, if his duties were sacrosanct, he was also absolutely uncompromising about his rights.

In the Sacristy on the massive chest of drawers in which he kept his vestments, beside the beautifully illuminated bible and discretely covered by a brownish cloth, he kept a scale of fees for all private functions such as masses, weddings, baptisms, funerals, etc., although he knew every line by memory.

On that dull and misty November day, as we said, the boys in primary five, given their unexpected day off, were playing within the cloister of the old monastery. The village streets were deserted and from the houses all around came a pungent aroma of roasted chestnuts.

Immersed as they were in their noisy games, they hardly noticed the little Sacristan moving among them with an anxious and worried look on his face, searching for the boys who usually rang the bells. But to no avail! Because these boys were at school that day! Suddenly he realised that he had blundered yet again.

Don Comodo emerged from the dimness of the staircase; having guessed the poor man's predicament, he began making threatening gestures even before he was anywhere near him.

"You ass... Imbecile! I just knew you'd lost your mind!"

The Sacristan, poor man, suffered memory lapses and was often overcome by an inexplicable sleepiness, so much so that he would often be found asleep on his cobbler's workbench.

"There is no time to lose, I can hardly ever trust you, can I?" shouted Don Comodo, pushing the poor man aside and calling round him the boys who were there playing, he asked:

"Who would like to ring the bells?"

"Me," answered our young boy, raising his hand. "Me, Don Comodo, me!"

To his great surprise our boy was chosen along with two others, and there and then the Sacristan led them to a room at the base of the bell tower and while disappearing by the Altar, he told them to wait there until he returned, adding "It is a funeral; funeral bells to ring!"

Five minutes later, an eternity for the boys, heavy footsteps on the stone floor of the church announced the arrival of the funeral cortege. The plain coffin, covered by a black drape, was placed in the middle of the floor in front of the Altar while a dozen or so people sat around in silence. It was obviously a poor funeral.

Dressed for the occasion, Don Comodo came in with the cortege, rushed into the Sacristy and the Sacristan, having rested the long Cross against the wall behind the Altar, was about to go to the boys to give them the signal when the Sacristy door screeched and Don Comodo reappeared, stopping him:

"Have they paid?" he asked.

"Yes." answered the Sacristan. "Ten lire."

"Good," said the priest.

Taking the money from his pocket, the Sacristan ran back into the Sacristy and handed it to Don Comodo. This was the minimum fee for a funeral and prescribed a brief benediction service, accompaniment of the cortege to the outskirts of the village, half a mile down the road and the ringing of bells until it reached the village square about a hundred yards down the narrow street from the church.

At the base of the bell tower the boys had been patiently waiting for their great moment and were by now getting bored. The place was quite creepy; all around lay broken dusty planks and benches, torn scarlet umbrellas, picture frames in a pile and angels with broken wings. The pungent aroma of incense lay as a condiment on top of the smell of dry rot and mould. They were not made to wait long as the Sacristan, reappearing, instructed them to ascend the staircase to the bells.

The inside of the bell tower resembled an upturned funnel into which the light in violent jets filtered from the summit and the wooden steps, blackened by time, climbed from landing to landing which got smaller towards the top.

With the confidence of a skilled climber, our boy was first to attack the climb and having reached the top landing, he launched himself at the clapper of the largest of the bells overlooking the little square in front of the church.

The benediction was short, as we can imagine, and it was not long before the little cortege appeared on the square and moved onward to the accompaniment of the strangest peal of bells ever heard.

At funerals it was generally a slow lugubrious tolling heard for miles, which froze the blood of the peasants in fields both near and far. But the boys, full of enthusiasm, had transformed it into a delightful lively and loud melody. The people were puzzled, asking each other what all this pealing meant and if by an unusual circumstance, they were spared a pause of ill-fated melancholy, the dead man was perhaps enjoying his last laugh.

The boys continued to ring with spontaneous new tunes and would have gone on for hours if the Sacristan had not appeared out of the mist, on the little road leading up from the square to the church, carrying the Cross on his shoulders. Don Comodo followed him absolutely speechless and gesticulating vehemently.

The boys who, from the top of the bell tower, were unable to see the stern expression on the face of the parish priest, thought it was the signal to stop and reluctantly but full of happiness and pride began to descend the long staircase anticipating the praises of Don Comodo whom, having reached its base out of breath, still in his white robes and his three cornered cap, stood there impassively.

Completing their descent, the boys found themselves face to face with Don Comodo who, far from dispensing praises, caught our boy by the jacket, shook him and administered two hearty slaps to his young face causing his ears to ring. At the same time, the other boys, having quickly sized up the situation, put on wings, running towards the exit like two frightened hens.

"We must have rung badly," thought the boy, while large tears came down his cheek.

"Stupid!... Stupid boys!... Idiots!" Don Comodo kept shouting, "You should have stopped ringing when we reached the Square; why did you not stop?"

"But nobody told us," murmured the boy, crying like a baby, somewhat relieved, "we did not know."

On hearing this Don Comodo, wearing a severe expression, turned around to face the poor Sacristan who, anticipating trouble had set himself at a distance with his back against the wall. He grabbed him by the collar and raising his right arm high in a threatening fashion, shouted "I should have known!... It's all your fault. Why did you not tell them?" In the squalor and dim light of the place, his arm and open hand seemed almost like an executioner's axe about to fall heavily on the face of the poor unfortunate man, when, as if held by a celestial force, it stopped and stood stiff and motionless for a few seconds. Don Comodo seemed to shiver and suddenly, turning around in anguish, humbly, his eyes to the heavens, he began to implore loudly, "Jesu... Sweet Jesus... Holy Mary... !" and crossing himself repeatedly he rushed towards the Sacristy, slamming behind him the heavy oak door in such a way as to shake the church in its foundations.

Four Plus Four Makes Eight

Four plus four makes eight.

There can be no doubt: it is a mathematical certainty which stands no contradiction and, if there were a need for a proof, you could not have found a better person to give it to you than Mr Peter Brucciani who, with this simple arithmetical operation and a philosophy based on this certainty, profitably succeeded in building a sizeable wholesale business selling ice cream, cigarettes, chocolate and biscuits. Not that he had discarded all the other operations; it was because it was the only one he knew.

He successfully conducted his business from the back room of the Crown Cafe, but the cafe itself was only a pretext to be able to operate his more profitable business, the wholesale trade in ice cream and tobacco at all times of the day, from seven in the morning to midnight, seven days a week right through the year. He made no profits from the cafe and apart from the fact that it suited him so well to keep it open for the obvious reasons, it was a sentimental object and an important part of his sociological and philosophical set up, where a single element amiss could have caused collapse. Truthfully, Peter Brucciani had no need for excuses, nor would he ever have thought of them. He was just doing what over the years came to him naturally and with all probability, he did not even know that the cafe was running at a loss. The whole complex grew and developed with its own momentum. This is what he had built up a little at a time, starting with this small cafe.

Four plus four was not just what it means: adding to eight, but a way of saying in Italian that things can be done in a flash: just like that!... Or that they happen in a flash, just as easy as that. It was a saying Peter Brucciani made his own, where the practical side of it, that is the addition itself, played a large part umpteen times each day.

Every morning for several hours, there was a continuous coming and going of Mobile Shops getting ready to shoot off in all directions with their fare: a number of young Italians just immigrated and a sprinkling of Scots and Irishmen, intent on replenishing their shelves with Peter's merchandise.

"Peter, it is such a lovely day; I think I shall be needing twenty-four gallons of ice cream.

"Peter, five thousand cigarettes and twelve gallons of ice cream, please."

"Good morning, Peter."

"Good morning."

"May I have ten gallons of ice cream and eight thousand cigarettes?..." and quick as a flash he and Nicky, his assistant, served them all.

"Peter, how much is my bill?"

"Just a minute." To add it all up, he would write down the price per gallon, sixteen shillings, twenty-four times one below the other and add it up.

"Peter, I haven't got enough money now, can I pay the rest tomorrow?"

"Yes, of course."

"If it's no bother, Peter, I'll have to pay it all in loose change."

"That's OK. Have you counted it?" he would ask, and throw the lot in a drawer, along with banknotes and occasionally some cheques.

"Peter my bill, please." He would quickly start another addition and, quick as a flash, pronto: the sum to pay. Quite often he used to stress that the family in Italy was very poor and could not afford to send him to school, that he had had to work from the age of seven and that he only spent one year at the elementary school. "I wish they had let me carry on, at least up to third or fourth year. I would have been able to read and write. But here I am... an illiterate."

To be illiterate does not mean that a man is not intelligent. He had not created an empire for himself from nothing! He did not use books or cash registers of any kind, yet he appeared infallible. He had devised a simple personalised accounting system as logical as "four plus four makes eight". On his desk, a four-legged table against the wall, among other things, there were two long wire nails on a wooden base on which he spiked scribbled envelopes of the kind used in the cafe for the sale of loose sweets. On one of the nails were the cash sales and on the other the credit ones. A large part of his own purchases were paid by cash; the reps would call and collect it in large bundles. The tobacco bills, from some of the largest tobacco companies in Britain and one or two other bills, were taken to his solicitors with his cheque book at each month's end. After a day or two the cheques were passed to Peter for his signature, which was like a cardiogram and quite impossible to imitate.

A glance at those envelopes would have left you puzzled. Not a vowel, consonant or number was recognisable. It was a handwriting invented and elaborated by Mr Brucciani and only he could read it. When someone called to pay a debt, he would sift through the pile and quickly fish out the right one, just like that: quick as a flash.

His customers kept him in good spirits. When someone wanted to buy a new sales van he would just nod: "OK. I'll lend you the money and you can pay it back out of ice cream sales. For the moment, we'll keep the van in my name if that's all right with you?" and in next to no time there was another mobile shop to be supplied with his merchandise.

This extraordinary man was a tireless worker. Sixteen hours a day he was to be found on his "Imperial" throne; a wooden chair set permanently near a rectangular table against the wall of the back shop.

As soon as all the vans had left for their sales pitches in the suburbs and surrounding villages and Nicky Rubettazzi had completed his round of deliveries to the hotels, Peter pulled the drawer out of the desk and overturned it on his glossy table-top which had been polished no one knows how often in order to keep it smooth.

Nicky was a young man of about twenty years of age, who had come to Scotland at the age of ten with his parents who had found work there. His full name was Nicola Rubetazzi and he was born in Tursi in the Province of Matera. Nicky was a jack-of-all-trades: the ice-cream man, the chauffeur, the barman and, like everyone else, he had great respect for Peter.

Peter Brucciani would therefore begin counting the money, a job that went on right through the rest of the day. First the ten pounds notes, then the fives and the single pound notes in piles of one hundred pounds sterling, all tied up with an elastic band. When only the pile of silver and copper coins remained, he picked them up with speedy fingers, placing them in ten-pound sterling piles, lined up like soldiers on parade.

At lunch time, having on purpose left a clear spot on the table large enough to place a plate, he cooked himself his favourite meal on the gas cooker: a large sirloin steak with mushrooms and boiled potatoes. He would then open a bottle of Chianti and start eating, but even during this well-earned spell, he had no peace. People kept popping in for this and that, some wanting tobacco, some ice cream. Others wanted to pay a debt... and he?... quick as a flash dealt with everyone without showing the slightest hint of annoyance.

It would be easy to call this man a sort of Scrooge, mean and stingy, but that would be far from the truth. In fact he was compassionate and very generous, as the numerous charity collectors who regularly passed by his back shop could testify. Where else could they get a large banknote every time they called? He was also compassionate with all sorts of people who called for a small loan, people whom he knew would never repay or probably would never see again. That he lived his life in that way was not of his choice, nor was he aware that there could have been a better one.

Was it a passion or just a habit?... None of these, actually. It was because only in that chair that he felt comfortable and proud, only on that chair he did not feel any sense of inferiority: there he felt like a king. Where else would he attract so much respect and popularity? He was not handsome, and he was slowly getting old; he did not, in short, cut a dashing figure and as for manners, they were anything but refined. His speech was atrocious. He spoke broad Scots with the strongest of Italian accents.

As we said, his back shop was the head office and he himself the clerk and the accountant. The door was always open, and most people who knew him would just enter whether he was there or not. Now and then the policemen on the beat, in a casual sort of way, would enter without saying a word and go straight to the large kettle continuously boiling on the stove, pick up a cup and make themselves a cup of tea while Peter was counting money. All those who entered, for business or just a visit, particularly some elderly Italians from the area, felt so much at ease in that back shop that they sat and waited quietly until Peter stopped, turned around and asked: "Beh..? Come va?.." (How are things with you). He filled two glasses of wine and chatted a little while. Just for a little while since he was so busy, as everybody knew. They would sit there quietly for hours without uttering a word.

He had this rare quality of making anyone feel at home, without any fuss or ceremony.

He was in his late sixties, this extraordinary man and that seat had become both his throne and his life. He occupied it seven days a week, twelve months a year.

His business had grown with him through thick and thin, reaching a turnover of three thousand pounds a day; a figure of which he was extremely proud. He had come a long way since being brought to Scotland from his small village in the Garfagnana as a boy of barely eight years old! So much progress in the making of ice cream! He used to tell his friends that in the beginning it was made in a tinned steel canister surrounded by ice and rock salt in a sawn-off beer cask.

"Now; look at these machines:.. In no time at all I can produce ten hundredweight. Very hygienic too. You see, the good quality milk is first boiled here, then the butter is added. See this machine? It costs more than my motor car. It is called a homogeniser. I can't understand it; they say it breaks the butter. Bah. Then it is cooled in these things that look like scrubbing boards and finally, after we put in the other flavouring ingredients like the vanilla, we freeze it and make the ice cream."

When admiring all those machines, his face was gleaming with pride and satisfaction. Nicky, the young immigrant, and Berty, the old faithful labourer who worked upstairs in the factory, kept it spotless. He could depend on them so much that he hardly ever went there, except when he wanted to show it to friends and visitors.

Undoubtedly, Peter Brucciani was a proud man. His only regret in life was not having been able to study a little longer, at least up to the third or fourth year at primary, because those who studied to that level could write and read, while he felt "like an ass". In his back shop, however, no one could make a fool of him, even if his broken accent and a poor range of vocabulary made it difficult for him to express himself.

For an illiterate man he had, it could be said, a personal magic and even an acute sense of diplomacy. As matter of fact, this man who handled such a great deal of cash, openly, taking a small fortune to the bank every day, had never been assaulted by crooks and robbers. Every afternoon, at about three o'clock, as regular as clockwork, he would go to the bank, two hundred yards away, loaded down with two large bags, one in each hand, weighing, perhaps half a hundredweight each, and every pocket bulging with bundles of banknotes, looking quite unconcerned.

I do believe it could have been the knowledge that once, in the past, he had reacted quite violently to someone who tried to rob him (in his youth he must have been a strong man), but primarily his diplomacy. Every year at Christmas, a profusion of gifts to everyone in authority, and police in particular, must have kept him well protected. Local small time crooks were well advised not to touch him. Then there was the car. Without being able to drive he would buy a new one every second year.

But, goodness me! It would quickly be covered in rust! However, the hand of providence came to his rescue: a police sergeant took it out for a drive every weekend and on his days off. The gentleman came in through the back door, stopped for a while on the doorstep, for Peter to finish counting or scribble. Having finished his chore, Peter would take the car keys from a nail on the wall above the table and hand them to him with very few words, just expressing his gratitude for the favour.

For a man who had no schooling, in my opinion, this amounted to high level diplomacy.

His only relaxation was a game of cards late at night, when he, myself and my friend Roberto Orlandi, who were often his partners, would sit down together. We would play for an hour or two, no more, and Peter always hated being disturbed when he was playing.

He would get very annoyed if Nicky came up from the bar to ask him something or other.

He was not even dull or insipid for his way of life! Not even a bore. Occasionally he would come out with some jokes and would laugh with that distinct rasping laugh of his which sounded like the regular beat of a large pendulum clock. He was always the one to control the conversation and jokes at will, being serious when he wanted to. Sometimes he would let us in on some of the sales reps' secrets. Indeed, they were things he ought not to have told me: "... and so, quick as a flash, he slapped his wife and she, quick as you like, threw the frying-pan at his head! Ha.. ha.. ha... "

His humour was not of the best but served in some way to break that dreadful monotony which, even if of his own choice, must have occasionally been a burden to him.

He had no family. At the age of fifty he married a young assistant in the shop, some thirty years younger than him. However, he did have many nephews, sons of his brother in a nearby town who rarely came to pay him a visit. Too busy studying.

Anne, his wife, was a very nice woman. She was of Irish stock and, at forty, she still looked attractive. She had a lot of respect for Peter, who could never believe she would have an affair, even though, some four or five years after their marriage they decided that Anne should move up to live on the second floor, leaving Peter on the first floor above the shop. She was often in the back shop and Peter would give her as much money as she wanted. Just like that!... without batting an eyelid.

Sometimes he would take her to business dances such as the ice cream alliance's, but the poor woman used to complain that they never went away for a holiday! How could he get away from his business?... His chair, or "throne" was the only place he felt relaxed, peaceful and free of any feeling of inferiority. Quite rightly, too. Sitting in his chair he could feel deservedly proud!

What a great pity, then, that a man of such calibre was destined to die, against his will, just like the rest of us poor mortals.

It happened unexpectedly.

One day, I and my friend Roberto, passed by his back shop to ask if Peter would like to come with us to the races. We were surprised to see one of his older nephews sitting on the famous chair, that well-worn royal throne, intent on counting the day's takings and Anne, Peter's wife, standing by the communicating door to the cafe.

"Where's Peter?..." we asked.

"Haven't you heard? He's been taken to hospital with a stroke. Fortunately, it's not too serious."

A few days later, my friend and I went to visit him in hospital. When we got there he was asleep, or was he?... He looked as if he had already departed: his breathing was raucous and he was snoring lightly. His face was gaunt and his eyes were sunken under blackened eyelids. We pulled out two chairs and sat in silence, not wanting to disturb him. However, he must have perceived our presence. He stopped the raucous noise and slowly opened his eyes. Having recognised us he put on, or rather, tried to put on his usual large smile. It was so pathetic that we felt shivers through our blood.

A while later he tried to laugh in his tick-tock way, while with great efforts, lifting himself from the pillow with his elbows, he tried to tell his best joke:

"Have... you... heard... " – his voice seemed to come from a hole in a large wooden cask – "have... you... heard... the... st... ory... about the Irish... man and... the... rabbi?"

It was quite piteous. He tried to laugh off his shame at having been caught in such an undignified position; his pride just could not allow it. The cough soon became quite hollow. He gave a sudden jerk and fell back on his pillow. He was dead!

As quick and as sure as "four plus four makes eight", he was dead!

The Coughing Flea

Back and forward, back and forward. The arguments would have never ended had not the Sergeant and two Carabinieri intervened. Even in the presence of the law, however, the insults flew from an even greater distance, from one side to the other. In fact those who had supposedly trespassed the boundary, that is to say the Grassano people, began vehemently to argue with the Sergeant from the Grottole Station who, in their opinion, had no right to be there and, in any case, the job of policing the festivities ought to be done by the Grassano police.

The Feast of Saint Anthony, the Abbot, began in this way every year, invariably with the early arrivals of the same people who, at daybreak, wanted to assert their ancient right on the one hand and, on the other, to protest at the vile usurpation of their claim to the Saint, arguing with each other over the best spot for the customary picnic, on the invisible boundary near the little Chapel.

Undoubtedly, the tumble-down chapel belonged to Grottole. Even the Carabinieri from Grassano who arrived a little later, confined themselves to their side of the border and acted with great discretion as if, truthfully, the entire process of policing the feast was not within their competence, avoiding stepping over the border in order not to offend the sensibilities of the Grottole people or their colleagues.

But who, using a little common sense, could have built that remote Chapel right on the village boundary, is a mystery.

"It was a man from Grassano who thought it was on our side," the Grassano people used to say.

"No; it was a man from Grottole who had his pigs cured of a terrible disease," said the Grottole people.

The Grassano people had tried several times asking the Provincial Authority to reset the boundary and had even lobbied Parliament. But all in vain. Their claim was partially supported by the chapel being only half an hour's walk from Grassano but nearly two hours from Grottole. No commission had ever had the courage to change things.

The chapel undoubtedly was in Grottole territory even if the attached building, two stables, with two rooms over, accessed by a long outside staircase, belonged to a man from Grassano who lived there and, in theory, was the Church Warden.

These arguments, which had continued since time immemorial, had created an unfriendly feeling between the two villages which, on the day of the Feast, assumed the proportions of a real war.

In the little chapel the saint slept all through the year, and on the day before the feast the women from the adjacent farmhouse came down to do some cleaning and to sweep down the cobwebs stretching right down to the pavement, the rest of the year nobody bothered.

The rustic simplicity of the facade showed signs of the age and was getting worse. The roughcast, peeling off all over, revealed the ancient stonework. At the level of the eaves, an arch of pink bricks supported a small bell, and two round windows at the side of the front door, highlighted the Altar of local stone. Inside, there was a smell of old lime mortar and mildew, while on the cracked, peeling plaster walls hung many articles of votive offering.

Saint Anthony, the Abbot, is acknowledged as the Patron Saint of Animals so, on his Feast Day no living creature but cats and chickens, animals which, seemingly, were not worth blessing, remained in the two villages. All other animals, except uncontrollable flocks, were dragged along the dirty mule tracks, across the murky stream, often in full flood, right up to the plateau in front of the chapel for the annual benediction. It was often the case that pigs in particular would be obviously reluctant to run the distance, giving rise to a liberal use of a stick, causing great laments and grunts of protest. But there was no resisting; with much pushing, kicking and thrashing, they all got up to the plateau.

In front of the little church, on top of a bare and bleak hill, situated between two streams, people were sitting all around with saddles, stools, mules, donkeys, sheep, goats and pigs, each claiming his territory to consume their picnic.

Having settled the early arguments, everything would run smoothly until the little bell rang the eucharist. Within this period, those related from one village and the other greeted each other with flasks and bottles of wine while the kids played together and followed the brass band which accompanied the collection of alms.

Don Comodo, the parish priest from Grottole, who officiated at the religious services by right, was meanwhile discussing the accounts and budgets with the organisers of the festivities and the carabinieri were taking refreshment in the stable next to the church which had been converted into a "Cantina", or wine shop for the occasion. This was the only advantage or profit from neutrality for the guardian of the church, who was serving everyone with a satisfied and pleasant smile.

The people wandered here and there and even concluded some business, such as the sale of a mule, but as soon as the little bell rang out, announcing the imminent end of the Mass, an iron curtain fell between the villages.

Two groups of youths immediately formed up in front of the church; one from Grottole and the other from Grassano, while a festival organiser carrying a ledger in his hands, adding up and rewriting figures, put up for auction the statue of the saint and the Baldachin, the rich silk and gold canopy used to shield the saint. The amount of grain bid would determine who won the right to carry the statue of the saint and the four poled umbrellas sheltering the priest and the dignitaries of Grottole, including the town crier. This chap, on those kind of occasions, was always found among the top brass of the village, causing great annoyance.

The bids went fast and furious:

"Two hundredweights!... "

"Three!... "

"Five!... "

"Ten!... "

"The statue should be carried on the shoulders of the Grottole men. It's traditional!" someone shouted.

"Let's wait till it comes out of the chapel."

"The auction for the right to carry the Baldachin is now over," the festival organiser announced. "The Grassano men will carry it to the first gate."

When the Mass ended, the Sacristan came out first raising high the wooden cross and a lay brother in a white tunic followed holding a red umbrella over the head of Don Comodo who, needless to say, hated this particular feast to distraction. One can well imagine with what kind of humour he conducted the proceedings. The statue followed. The saint looked completely estranged and uninterested; his pious face distanced and indifferent, seeming neither to approve nor disapprove.

When the fireworks began to go off with a deafening noise, it became quite impossible to control the mules and donkeys who began braying at full blast. While the women knelt and the youths continued to argue, the saint, standing on a table at the church door, was waiting patiently for things to get sorted out.

Don Comodo was trying very hard to remain calm and Socrates, the town crier, kept trying hard to reassure him, standing close to him, as though to offer protection. Socrates, known in the village by this nickname because he had a habit of philosophising, was also termed a busybody by the village gentry from whom he gained the demeaning name: "The Coughing Flea", all because they could not keep him at a distance and because, when they were having their evening walk in the village square, he would intrude in their discussion, always insisting on putting things right. For example: when they said that an ass is an ass, he would intervene by saying that it was the product of cross breeding between a horse and a mule. They did not like it and quickly moved away whispering to each other; "The Coughing Flea."

Don Comodo would have preferred to keep him away even if subjected to a few more pushes in the mayhem, but on this occasion good sense and prudence had made an alliance and he let himself be protected without protesting further. As a matter of fact, when tolerated, Socrates stuck to people like a flea and, several times during the procession, Don Comodo had to push him away. Seeing as he was as tall and dried-out as a bamboo cane, this almost caused the poor man to lose his balance and fall over.

The procession arrived at the first gate moving at a slow and laboured pace. A table had been set up there, on which the statue was to be placed for the resumption of the auction.

It was at this point that things began to go from bad to worse. The auction bids restarted and when some of the group said that they were prepared to go above ten bushels of wheat, the Grottole chaps began arguing among themselves. The richer ones played the show-off, accusing the others of betraying the cause, but when some of the other youths who were prepared to continue the auction joined the group, those who could not make up their minds left the scene.

The bids re-started fast and furiously: Grassano offered twelve and Grottole replied with fifteen. The honour of the village was at stake! When the bidding got to twenty bushels, the arguing gave way to insults and finally to violence. All around the statue things looked like a battlefield. It all started with a push, then a punch. A cousin came in to help relatives, someone who had a stick used it heavily on the head of the next chap; the Grassano boys swore they had put in the final bid and won the right to carry the statue. Soon punches, kicks and clubs were flying in all directions, and while the women shouted in terror, the carabinieri threatened to make arrests in the name of the law, themselves sustaining a few kicks and punches.

Don Comodo took refuge among the bandsmen, closely followed by the town crier who stuck to him like glue, keeping close enough to annoy him and throw doubt on his role as protector. Those with cuts and bruises ran to the church to get bandaged and while the fight went on, the statue, laid on an insecure table, swayed in all directions. A certain calm was re-established when the Carabinieri from Grassano also arrived following heartfelt pleas from some of the dignitaries and festival organisers. The bids restarted in earnest:

"Twenty-one... "

"Twenty-two... "

"Twenty-four... "

"Twenty-six... "

When it reached thirty, the Grassano boys, some of whom had bleeding noses, gave up, leaving the Grottole boys, in their opinion, with the hot poker in their hands.

The procession continued as if nothing had happened and once it reached the site of a large steel cross at the edge of the plateau, Don Comodo dispensed the benediction of the animals, who, unaware of the privilege, continued to bray and roar.

When the saint returned to the church, most people had already left for their respective villages, singing the melodious country songs at the tops of their voices, accompanied by the music of rustic concertinas, flutes and castanets, while flasks of wine were passed back and forth from one rider to the other. Half-way there was the shady glade where the usual swings were put up for the children and the dances were held. It was also the ideal place and situation for the start of romantic affairs, with the go-betweens doing great business.

Meanwhile, the saint, stripped of all the offers of money pinned on his red mantle and staff, was placed in his glass cubicle inside the disputed old chapel.

With the mules ready in front of the church, Don Comodo, the festival organisers, some gentry and the carabinieri came out in the open air for the return to the village.

Closing the door with the heavy, rusty key, and having spotted a man on a horse with a bandaged head, Don Comodo began mumbling:

"Shame;... all so disgusting!... " However, Socrates, who as usual found himself always with the top brass as if that was his proper place (and no one was prepared to get rid of him), interrupted:

"But Don Comodo, I beg you pardon, this is surely just another way of praying. You see; faith brings them here, faith makes them offer their precious wheat, and faith makes them fight. Religion and tradition; a funny mix. The important thing is that they believe in God. It is just another way of praying."

One of the dignitaries stretched out his arm to push the poor chap away and silence him but Don Comodo, who was left dumbstruck by those words, his mouth open and the chapel keys dangling from his hand, stopped him. He would have embraced the town crier had it not looked silly in front of all the others and for a moment he wished his faith was as staunch as that.

Surely, this "this coughing flea" ought to have been made provost of the village, and got him to preach in church every Sunday!

Fried Fish and Bitter Bread

Mr Carciofo, although well advanced in age, nearer sixty than fifty, still sported a full head of thick, curly, black hair which framed a round face which had not lost its youthful appearance. Long sideburns came down over his cheekbones in a perfect match with his bushy eyebrows, fleshy lips, a dimpled chin and dark eyes which, alas, no longer sparkled.

Mr Carciofo was a most unhappy man. His unhappiness was well deserved, for it had been caused by his own stubbornness.

"A man warned in time... " But he would not listen.

"Good heavens: marry your shop assistant? No!... for goodness sake," all his friends said.

Worse still was the effect on his poor old mother: "No!... No... you are mad!" she shouted when she heard. "A woman thirty years younger than yourself? A divorcee? A loose woman, as everybody knows and a Protestant into the bargain!... You are going crazy!... "

Some time later the poor woman died of a broken heart.

"Poor old dad... " his daughter commiserated. Some time later she married an American soldier and went off to the States. "You will live to regret it."

On the wedding day he wanted to have a reception but all his friends declined. Baroncini alone agreed to act as best man at the wedding which took place in the Town Hall. All the others, it seems, had good excuses for staying away.

And now what?... There are timely proverbs such as "you have made your bed, so now you must lie on it". When you have been well warned, advised, appealed to by friends and relatives, yet stubbornly "take the plunge", you only have yourself to blame and it is only right that you should suffer the consequences.

Nobody, Carciofo was sure, was going to feel sorry for him, more likely they would split their sides laughing: "... Told you so" – "Remember my advice? – Poor old fool."

This is why those eyes, once so proud and glowing, were getting dimmer and dimmer day after day; the light seemed to have gone out of them altogether.

He was unaware, but his efforts in trying to look normal made him introverted and unsociable, so much so that he could no longer look into the eyes of his friends who, though they had spurned and criticised his marriage, still retained a certain esteem and respect for him.

Carciofo began to suspect that they were aware of his unhappiness and, right or wrong, he thought he saw an ironical smile on every face. In any case, sooner or later everybody would know, because he thought he would not be able to hide his misery much longer and that his despair would burst forth for all to see.

It was nearly midnight when he got home from the shop, tired and dejected, not as much from his work as from the prospect of another sleepless night, endless tirades from his wife and the impossibility of making her stop or keep quiet.

When he got into the house he thought she was asleep but as soon as he opened the bedroom door she turned to face him with a sneering smile and a challenging laugh of satisfaction for herself that surprised Mr Carciofo.

"Know what I am doing tomorrow?... I am off... I am leaving you."

"Oh well... " replied Carciofo by now quite used to the threats.

"You can pretend as much indifference as you wish, but tomorrow I would like to see your face when you discover I am serious. Pretend you do not care, but I will be away never to come back."

"All right... all right..." Mr Carciofo kept repeating drowsily, his eyes half asleep.

He was so tired and sleepy, he felt like he was being tortured. He undressed as in a trance and got into bed. He was asleep in no time while his wife went on telling him what she would do next morning; that she would go far, far away where he would never find her; away from his stinking smell of fish and chips.

Completely mentally and physically exhausted, he never heard a word. When she became aware of his state of oblivion she felt cheated; she shook him by the shoulders.

"Sleeping, are you?... Sound asleep?... Did you hear what I said?" He sat up with a jerk, "I heard... I heard..." he lied.

But she was not going to give up. She was unable to sleep, for she knew what she said was true and she could not wait for daylight or for him to leave for the fish market.

A few more shakes and thumps on the back and Carciofo got up, and half staggered into the sitting room to sleep there. He woke quite soon and, try as he might, he could not get to sleep again. At seven o'clock he pressed the button on the alarm clock to stop it ringing, rose and got ready to go to the fish market as he did every morning.

After putting on his old overcoat and working hat out of habit, the later quite greasy where it went round his head, he opened the door and made his way down the staircase to the garage which was at the rear of a shabby looking apartment building in a street dimly lit by gas street lamps.

Mr Carciofo hardly remembered anything of the past night; he only knew she had been ranting on at him. However he was now quite used to her jibes. His attempts at reasoning with her had had no effect and he had resigned himself, more out of exhaustion than anything else, to turning a deaf ear. There were times when he felt he could have shut her mouth for good. Umpteen times he had told her he was sorry, very sorry. For the sake of peace and tranquillity he promised to return to her ways in the shop, that he would give her all the money she wanted and he even told her he loved her. He would do anything to go back to the peaceful kind of life he enjoyed when she worked in the shop acting as if everything belonged to her.

"I was right; I know I was right," he kept telling himself – but this was atrocious. How could he allow things to go like that?... At the cash desk and in the shop she had become the boss. Every day at closing time he found the cash drawer empty; she needed one thing after another. She even claimed access to his savings book. It was just as well that neither he nor his father – God bless his soul – had ever put much money in the bank, to avoid paying taxes; she was very disappointed to find so little in the bank book and he, taking a cue from his wife's fortunate discovery began to give her a discreet, or so he thought, lesson in economy.

"My dear," he said, "we are happy, happily married and you have now become the boss both at home and in the shop, but we just cannot go on like this. I consider you are now well stocked with clothes, toiletries and the like, so, from now on, if you don't mind, I don't want you to take money from the cash drawer. Instead, every week I shall give you all the housekeeping money you need."

How he wished now he had not spoken! Had he but known how she would react!

"So... You want to go on treating me as a shop assistant... Is that what you want?"

"No. No... " he said apologetically in a humble tone. "It is just that I have to know just how much comes in and how much goes out."

"It is not that at all. It is because you always want to be the boss. Why did you marry me, eh?" She was becoming uncontrollable and started throwing things on the floor.

"I'm still to get a wage packet... is that it?"

"No... no... of course not!" he kept repeating. "Absolutely not!"

She took off her white overcoat and tossed it on the floor.

"I am still your shop assistant; that's what I am; and since that is what I am, there, there, take it. I resign."

Pale with rage, she ran into the back shop with Carciofo in pursuit trying to calm her down. She picked up her handbag, flung on her coat and rushed through the back door hurling insults.

"You lousy old miser... you filthy rascal... You blackguard."

"For heavens sake, come back! What's it all about... where are you going? Come back," poor Carciofo begged and cursed, all in vain.

That she did not love him, he knew all too well. But surely they could have come to an understanding such that they could have had a peaceful and contented life. At heart he was still fond of her, but for the love of God, why should she attack him in such a disgusting way, and for such a small matter?

If it was but a small matter for Carciofo, for her, of whom the general opinion was that she had married him for his money, it was a great tragedy. She was disillusioned.

For three whole weeks Carciofo tried to pacify her, offering all the money he possessed; his savings and bank accounts, meagre as they were, and all he had in his pockets, especially when, crouched in bed, she denied his marital rights. What hurt him most, however, were her crude insults and endless tirades when he got home from the shop late at night after a hard day's work. Having then exhausted all arguments to make her see reason, he resigned himself to suffering her anger passively. He adopted unconsciously the melancholy look now so evident in those dark eyes that were gradually growing dimmer and made him go about as though in a trance, doing things without knowing he was doing them.

"You wish to buy me, is that it?" she sneered when he tenderly offered her money. She would grab hold of it and turn away. "I take it because what is yours is mine, but my body I sell to whoever I wish."

"Then why did we get married? I offer you everything. Is it my soul you want?" Carciofo shouted one night out of his mind and completely enraged.

"Your soul can be sent to the devil," she said calmly taking the money.

Later Carciofo consoled himself with the thought that since he had not murdered her that night he was unlikely ever to do so. He knew she regretted having married him. It had seemed a good move to her at the time, but that paltry bank account and being forbidden the till were all that was needed to make her realise her mistake. Imagine her staying one more day in that house after discovering how she had been deceived on money matters.

As soon as she heard the door close behind her husband on the way to the market, she jumped out of bed with a self-satisfied smile. Humming to herself as she got ready to go out, she flung some clothes into a suitcase, phoned for a taxi, and then hurried downstairs to wait for it.

Meanwhile Carciofo had reached the garage, unlocked it and, still in pitch darkness, sat at the steering wheel and switched on the car headlights.

Before he could start the engine the short, fat figure of Tony Di Giorgio appeared, on the cadge as usual. The sheepskin jacket he habitually wore made him even stouter. After a brief greeting, he waited to shut the garage door when Carciofo had driven the car out, then sat down beside him without a word.

This was a routine that had gone on for years. Di Giorgio did not own a car and could not drive, so he had got into the habit of cadging a lift to the fish market every morning. His home was quite near but his shop – a fish and chip shop like Carciofo's – was about a mile away.

For some time now Carciofo had hated the sight of him. Admittedly it was not unusual for them to make the five-mile journey to the market without exchanging a word; but for some time past – since he had married Nancy – Carciofo thought he had noticed on Di Giorgio's face a sly, enigmatic smile, staring at him in a self-satisfied kind of way.

It had been raining all night, a fine, slow, persistent rain which collected soot from the air and deposited it on streets, walls and shop-windows, spreading a sharp smell of burnt ash, like when a chimney fire has been put out.

Here and there, on blocks of flats streaked and blackened by the filth, a few lighted windows could be seen; while on the pavements, here and there, some men made their way to work. On the main road gas lamps were replaced by orange-red-coloured fog lights which cast blood-red gleams on window panes and tram lines. At the stops stood workmen awaiting their transport, silent shadows on a background of smog-covered walls.

Carciofo was driving along absent-mindedly, so he hardly noticed they had reached the river, a short distance from the market. A whitish mist skimmed the water between the two river banks. He pulled up before they got to the bridge and parked the car.

At the entrance to the market – a Victorian structure with a huge arch supported by steel pillars – the two men went their separate ways to make their purchases.

The market was very crowded. Carciofo met several friends and fellow-countrymen but was not in the mood to chat long with anyone.

After ordering his requirements he felt he needed to be alone. He was heavy-eyed and longed to sleep, so he went out to the car and fell fast asleep as soon as he leaned back on the headrest. He had been asleep for half an hour or so when he heard a knock on the car window. It was his friend Baroncini who, by chance, had parked nearby.

"Hallo, Frank, what's the matter, you're asleep."

"OK, OK," replied Carciofo. "Just a bit tired."

"Let's go along to Cooper's. A wee walk and a nice coffee will put you right."

Cooper's cafe in St Enoch's Square was the daily haunt of the Italians who frequented the fish market. Immediately after making their purchases they would gather in one corner of the huge saloon to drink strong black coffee made Italian-style in a grand "Pavoni" machine shining with ornamental brass. There they would talk and gossip about their own and other people's affairs in a mixture of languages – Italian, Anglicised Italian, Scotticised Italian – with loud bursts of laughter and joking remarks, just like in bars at home in Italy.

Di Giorgio was there too, waiting inevitably for a lift back to Paisley on the outskirts of Glasgow where, like Carciofo, he lived and practised his trade. Baroncini went to the counter and ordered two coffees, and he and Carciofo sat down a little apart from the others. While the latter were loudly discussing the tax system and tax-evasion, Carciofo was idly sipping his coffee. Suddenly he turned pale as wax, let the cup fall from his hands fortunately onto an empty chair – and made a mad frantic rush towards the exit, leaving everybody open-mouthed. Running all the way he got to his car and drove at a furious speed, jumping traffic lights, to his house. He dashed up the stairs two at a time and burst into the sitting-room. A disorderly scene told the whole story – shirts, coats, handbags strewn on the floor and the settee overturned. There was no doubt about it: she had gone.

Tearing his hair with both hands he fell down in a faint.

When he came to, he looked about the room confused, grabbed hold of a chair and got to his feet. His temples were throbbing and he had a dry, bitter taste in his mouth. After staggering around for a bit he realised what had happened. Swearing hoarsely in his violent rage he seized anything within reach and hurled it against the wall. Then he burst into tears and, still cursing and lamenting, ended up on all fours behind the overturned settee.

Suddenly he thought he heard a knock on the door and stopped to listen, he knew it was not her. The knocking became louder but he made no move. Then grimacing with pain and his eyes still moist he stood up, sat down motionless and silent on a chair and listened to the knocking until it stopped. Going to the window he peeped out from behind the curtains: it was Di Giorgio.

"That carping runt," Carciofo muttered. "All he wanted was a good laugh."

Trying to compose himself he considered what to do next. He must at all costs track her down. He went into the bathroom and put his head under the cold water tap. In doing so he gave the wall a kick, and the pain this caused seemed to sharpen his senses.

After changing hurriedly he rushed down to the street where he had parked the car. The first thing he must do was to look for her at her sister's house, not that he expected to find her there, but maybe he could get a clue whether Nancy's sister and her husband were in on the plot.

They lived in a tenement building – one of those long rows of identical gloomy rented houses that formed a dismal, distressed area of the town. The entrance was through a narrow passage covered with rude graffiti, and four flights of stairs with dark landings led up to the fourth floor. Some of the steps were filthy with urine and vomit, a strong smell of beer assailed the nostrils, while communal toilets on the landings gave off a disgusting stench.

Carciofo knocked hard on the door. Jimmy his brother-in-law – an unemployed and shady character – came to open it. "Frank!" he exclaimed on seeing him. "Has something happened?"

"You know fine what has happened," Carciofo replied, "Where's Nancy?"

"Nancy? She's certainly not here."

"I know she's here," insisted Carciofo; pretending to be certain of it. "Don't play the fool."

Susan, Nancy's sister, put her head round the half-open door, angry but pleased at the same time.

"So, she has left you," she shouted, "and high time too, poor thing! Who could put up with a stinking miser like you? She did wrong to marry you, and she was quite right to leave you."

"It's you who're a stinking pair," Carciofo interrupted her, making for the stairs. "It's obvious from the kind of place you live in – a pigsty," he shouted when half-way down.

He went round the pubs she used to frequent before he married her, making enquiries, offering the barmen tips for any information. He was a pitiful sight, downcast and dejected.

Four days passed without success. His shop stayed shut, and Di Giorgio was happy to take over Carciofo's regular customers.

Everybody knew about it now; someone, sooner or later, would give him a clue. "Why don't you go to the police?" suggested one barman.

Carciofo didn't reply. Instead, he dressed in his best one night and went to see Charlie Zaccatini. Charlie ran a cafe in the centre of Glasgow frequented by waiters and other young Italians who were recent immigrants to Scotland. Among them were some who had finished their work-contracts and were now free to look for a place of their own to set up in. People knew that Charlie, with his many contacts, acted as middleman.

Charlie had heard of Carciofo's misfortune and felt sorry for him. Carciofo asked him if he knew anyone who would rent his business, telling Charlie he was desperate and needed time off to search for his wife "to the ends of the earth."

Zaccatini introduced him to a young man of about thirty, a native of Abruzzo. "My parents came from Molise," Carciofo informed him.

"Then we're fellow countrymen," said the young man. "Which part?"

"Campobasso province."

"My name is Di Prospero, Michael Di Prospero."

"I am Frank Carciofo."

"So you'd like to rent me your restaurant?"

"It's not a restaurant, it's a fish and chip shop."

"That doesn't matter, as long as it's a business."

Before parting they agreed to meet again next day, when Carciofo would take him to Paisley to see the shop.

Having been shut for about a week it was full of stale air and smelled of burnt fat and frying. Carciofo apologised and sorrowfully explained the reason – how he was now on his own, his daughter by his first wife had married and gone to live in America, while both his own parents were dead.

"It's barely four months since I got married again and I could have done without this blow; it's destroying me, I'm desperate."

"You must put a brave face on things," said Di Prospero, vexed.

By now it was lunchtime. Carciofo admitted that he hated eating alone and invited Di Prospero to join him for lunch at a nearby restaurant.

While they were waiting to be served, a travelling salesman of vegetable oils who supplied Carciofo among others, entered the restaurant.

"What! Mr Carciofo," he exclaimed. "I thought you were on holiday, at Blackpool!"

"No, I've shut up shop for a few days – for other reasons."

"I mentioned Blackpool because I thought I saw your wife there – at the Wellbeck Hotel. I must have been wrong."

"At the Wellbeck Hotel?" Carciofo exclaimed.

When the traveller went off to take a seat, Carciofo beckoned to Di Prospero, paid and made his excuses to the waiter who had arrived with the food and, followed by the young man, hurried out of the place.

"I'm off to Blackpool."

"I'll get a tram home, don't worry."

"I would like you to come along with me – please: I need company. Please!" Carciofo begged.

"But it's such a long way," the other protested.

"Please! We'll be back by tonight. You can help with the driving." Reluctantly Di Prospero agreed and got in beside Carciofo who set off at full speed.

The old main road between England and Scotland was very busy, making overtaking difficult. But after a journey of well over two hundred miles without a stop they reached Blackpool just as it was getting dark. The autumn display of the famous "Illuminations" was on, and the whole place was ablaze with lights and merry-go-rounds. Even the tramcars were decorated with coloured lanterns.

The Wellbeck, at one end of the long, glittering sea-front, was one of the town's biggest hotels.

Carciofo parked the car, a short distance from the brightly lit entrance and sat on at the steering-wheel. This seemed very puzzling to Di Prospero, and after ten minutes he asked the reason for the delay, surprised that Carciofo did not go into the hotel for his wife. He just gazed fixedly at the doorway and entrance-hall, where people kept coming in and out. Nearly an hour went by and Carciofo, teeth clenched, still made no move except for an occasional trembling.

"Why," repeated Di Prospero, beginning to get worried, "don't you go in and look for her? – It seems so odd." But Carciofo appeared not to be listening.

"I would rather not have got mixed up in private matters like this. I've half a mind to go and take a train home."

At that moment Carciofo suddenly shook as if he had taken a shivering turn.

"There she is!" he cried. "That's her coming out!"

"Where? Which one is her?" Di Prospero asked, curious.

"That one in the blue coat, she's coming out," he said, pointing to a young-looking woman, fair, thirtyish and shapely. She took a taxi which made off towards the town centre.

After smartening himself and smoothing his thick hair with his fingers Carciofo strode towards the hotel, leaving Di Prospero open-mouthed. At the reception desk he nonchalantly enquired about his wife who, he explained, had arrived a few days ago and was awaiting him.

The clerk looked up a register and told him that his wife was in a single room, Number 312. Carciofo paid for a transfer to a double room, then asked if she was in. The clerk glanced at the large key-rack. "No, she must have gone out;" and after checking the identity of the enquirer he handed Carciofo the keys of Room 312.

Meanwhile Di Prospero, uneasy, had got out of the car and was pacing up and down the pavement, a prey to all sorts of nervous fears. He began to think that Carciofo had taken leave of his senses and was waiting there in his wife's room in order to give her a beating or even to stab her. He had almost decided to leave the place but curiosity made him linger. Anxious as he was, he would have liked to know the outcome of the whole affair. If he had seen the police arrive he would have made a hasty retreat.

More than twenty minutes had passed – it seemed ages – when he caught sight of Carciofo hurrying out of the hotel, looking furtive.

On reaching the car Carciofo threw a parcel onto the back seat, took the wheel and was about to drive off without Di Prospero. The latter, enraged, caught up with him.

"Here, what's going on? You're not trying to leave me here? What have you been up to?"

"Nothing. Get in," said Carciofo and drove off at speed.

Di Prospero turned round and glanced at the package on the back seat. He could not suppress a cry of astonishment: the package had come undone and loads of large-denomination banknotes could be seen through the torn paper wrapping.

"Heavens above; have you stolen it?" the young man exclaimed.

"Stolen my foot," Carciofo retorted. "It's my money; money well earned."

"And what about your wife? I thought you were so broken-hearted."

Carciofo's face saddened: he bit his lip and made no reply.

When they were halfway home he let Di Prospero take the wheel.

To the young man he appeared to grow sadder by the minute. His lack of concentration had been making his driving erratic and dangerous.

When he settled on the passenger seat he was very nervous and biting his lips as if holding back a sob. Depression was remorselessly eating at his soul.

"You know how much money is in there?" he said to keep the conversation going.

"How much?" Di Prospero asked.

"Ten thousand pounds!" To an astonished Di Prospero he continued: "Enough to buy a couple of palaces in Italy. To save that money my father had to endure humiliations and tribulations of all kinds. He had to work hard up to midnight seven days a week and often deal with some rowdy and hard to please customers. He used to say: 'It's not just frying fish, you know; it's the bitter pill you have to swallow at times, being in a foreign land.' My father, God bless his soul, drowned in the sinking of the ill-fated "Arandora Star", a ship carrying Italian internees to Canada. It was sunk by German submarines in the Atlantic. Before he was taken away by the police my father said to me: 'There, my son, this represents all my sweat and sacrifice,' showing me the hiding place. I have sweated into so many shirts and swallowed many bitter pills, so be careful, do not waste it.'" After a short pause Carciofo continued:

"You know, I left it there under the floorboards untouched. I felt so shy. I felt I was going to touch something sacred. That is why I had to find her and retrieve the money." His voice hovered half-way between anger and emotion. He paused yet again, wiping a tear from his eyes, then continued:

"I was quite fond of her, you know. We could have had a good life together. She will regret it when she finds herself very lonely. As lonely as I was before I married her; after the death of my wife Rosa, God bless her soul. She will taste the anguish of loneliness." After a long silence he went on: "She was not a bad soul, you know... but she should not have done this to me." He was sobbing and stuttering. "She should not have done this to me..."

His eyes were wet and his voice quite inaudible.

When they reached Glasgow they went first to Di Prospero's lodgings. As he got out of the car the young man asked: "Are we still going ahead with the rental of the shop?"

"We'll see... We'll see," replied Carciofo.

When Carciofo got to his house he felt a chill run through his bones. He fixed the floorboard and set the settee upright. Nancy's portrait on the wall was still smiling, but he knew she would by now be crying in that hotel bedroom and full of regrets. But punished, just as she deserved. He looked at a photo of his late wife Rosa; he felt forlorn and lonely. In bitter despair he hurled the package on the floor and, hiding his face in his hands, slumped on the settee and burst into a flood of tears and wracking sobs.

"Rosa!... Where are you, Rosa?"

The Search

"Dear Marcantuono,
        Always at that blessed farm: I have got a registered letter for
        you. Now, if you want it you must go personally to the Post
        Office to get it.
                                    Signed: Alighiero the Postman."

"Five times I have been here, I am absolutely fed up," the poor
postman lamented hopping along like a gazelle from one door to the
other in the neighbourhood.
        "A registered letter!"
        "It may well be some sort of summons."
        "Not at all, the postman says it comes from America."
In no time everyone knew it. A registered letter from America:
        "It could be from that fellow who was here last year."
        "Who?... "
        "The chap who was thought to be a criminal lawyer in New York
or Chicago, don't you remember?"
        "Of course; it may well be. He gave himself so many airs. He
looked like a feathered peacock!"
        For heaven's sake! All the neighbours knew of the blessed
registered letter, giving themselves imagining all sort of things not
without a hint of malice. But Marcantuono, blessed be God, unaware
of the commotion the letter had caused, happily pressed on with the
harvest; there at the farm with everybody, even the in-laws, manning
the big combined harvester and sacking the wheat to be loaded on the
incoming lorry. About the in-laws they would say: "Of course, they
are old and not of much help; but what would they do at the village,
they would be bored to death," on this, Marcantuono, his wife and
children, ten year-old Marietta and thirteen year-old Carminuccio all
agreed.

It was like a fiesta; especially when the big lorry came to collect the bags of wheat for the pasta factory.

"How many bags?"

"Sixty."

"Are you sure? You look as if you are still asleep; are you sure?..."

"Yes... yes; of course I am sure. I am not stupid," the boy remarked quite crossly and with conviction.

Hi son was indeed a very good boy. He had passed his third year exams at secondary school with good marks, which made him cultured enough to take the mickey out of his father occasionally. Imagine! He had been studying algebra and the square root!

"The square root?" his father would comment, "I've never heard of a square root - what kind of tree would that be?"

The kids laughed, even if they knew that he kept repeating that phrase just to see them laugh.

"They are numbers! Very complicated numbers, papa, not tree roots." Mr Marcantuono wanted nothing to do with complex numbers. For him, if one sows he will harvest; if he sets a vine he will fill his cellar with wine.

"And if one goes to church every Sunday he will eventually go to Paradise," Costanza, a good Christian, used to add at dinner on Sundays when they were not at the farm, but in their recently completed handsome new cottage with the mechanical arthesian well just there on the doorstep.

The Marcantuonos, both husband and wife preferred that cottage to the house in the village. Not the kids, though, who could not wait for the time to return to their friends there. So to please them, and since the tomato fields were not ready to be harvested, they all made their way into the village in the Ducato van through the fresh, clear air of a late afternoon.

As soon as she had opened the front door, Costanza headed straight for the kitchen.

"Mother! Mother! There is a note; a note on the floor behind the door," Marietta shouted greatly excited.

"A note? What is in it? Go on read it!" Costanza ordered, full of anxiety.

"It is from Alighiero the Postman. He says there is a registered letter for us at the post office."

"A registered letter? Goodness me... what can it be? Quick, call your father."

Marietta rushed to the big hatch which led to the garage via a flight of wooden steps and began shouting in a dither: "Papa... Come up, quick... come up!"

"What?... What is it?"

Father and son ascended the ladder to the dining room in great haste.

"A registered letter?... Where is it?"

"At the Post Office. It says if we want it we must go there to collect it."

And away they went in full flight of fancy wondering what could it be. Who had sent it? Maybe the Tax Office... the Town Hall... or the bank? Late into the night they kept guessing, accompanied by jokes from the kids and occasional worrying comments from the father. "We have nothing to fear," Costanza stressed reassuringly. "Why should we worry. Off to bed all of you. We shall find out tomorrow."

As soon as they put their heads on their pillows, the kids fell sound asleep. But not Marcantuono. He tossed and turned in his bed which was as big as a field of beans. Costanza pretended to sleep to avoid encouraging him to worry more. Occasionally she would ask: "Are you asleep yet?" and he would answer with a curse.

He would curse quite often, not out of conviction but simply as a habit just to give vent to his nerves: "To hell with this and to hell with that!..."

When daylight came he had not closed an eye, while the kids were still fast asleep. He had barely got up and dressed when up he went to Carminuccio's room.

"Get up! Come on, up you get!"

"What time is it?"

"Never you mind. Come on, get up!"

The boy opened his eyes, gave a long yawn and glanced at the clock. He gestured in annoyance and pushed his head under the sheets. "Seven o'clock; it's not fair." But his father pulled the blankets off him and there was no resisting. He had to get up.

"We need to go to the post office for this blessed registered letter," his father concluded apologetically.

"But the Post Office does not open until nine o'clock."

"We'll walk slowly," his father replied, strangely cheerful.

Would that big clock on the mantlepiece never go any faster? Seven thirty... eight... eight thirty... tick tock... tick tock... Costanza opened the front door wide to clean the steps. The whole neighbourhood was out in the street, anxious to discover what was in the letter.

"Good morning, are you back?... Have you picked up that letter from America?"

"From America! Dear Lord," and away she rushed to give the news to her husband, sitting in the dining room watching the clock.

"Ah!... All this worrying. What can it be?"

"It will be from the lawyer."

There was no urgency any more. When they all got together they had a good laugh.

Holy Mother of God!... All that anxiety!... But why registered? Mystery was now creeping on the scene and slowly but surely, a compelling desire to know its contents.

Half an hour before it was due to open, father and son were in front of the little post office, anxiously pacing up and down the cobbled street. It was a beautiful clear morning with vibrantly fresh air. The sun was already high in the sky spreading its golden veils on the ancient hill which had earlier shed wheat and barley, gently caressing the silvery olive tree and the mellow vine.

Finally the staff arrived. After a ten minute wait which seemed an eternity, they opened the door to the public. Cautiously the two entered:

"Good morning." No one answered. The staff were actually discussing the latest official business in a low voice. A young lady in a grey overcoat came to the counter.

"Good morning, Miss. We have come for the registered letter."

"Ah!... Let's see." She picked up the letter from a drawer. "What is your name, please?"

"My name is Marcantuono, Miss. You know me, I am Marcantuono."

"There is a difficulty, my dear Mr Marcantuono. The letter is in fact addressed to Marcantonio. We discovered it only yesterday. If we go by regulations we should return it to the sender.

"But it is mine. It comes from my cousin in America."

"I said, my dear Marcantuono, we should send it back, but... "

"... but it is mine."

"Let me finish, please," continued the lady in the grey dress. "In normal circumstances we could not give it to you. But because you are well known in the village and also at the Post Office, we may be able to let you have it if you can provide us with a declaration on a three-thousand lire official taxed form stating that you are the person to whom the letter is addressed and that you have clear knowledge of its source and sender. It will need to be countersigned by two witnesses."

"Well," sighed Marcantuono with relief. "We shall come back. Good morning to you."

They were hardly out on the cobbled street when Marcantuono started his usual mild swearing: "Why Marcantonio, eh? Why... He knows damned well that our name is Marcantuono, not Marcantonio."

"But Papa, Marcantuono is dialect, in Italian it is Marcantonio."

"Yeah... Yeah... Yeah... The same thing. You don't like your own name any more?"

He was taking his anger out on the poor boy. They were on the verge of a silly argument.

Meanwhile they were nearing the tobacconist's shop.

Mr Collato, a good man with a pension, was temporarily minding his son's shop. Business being slack, he was sitting on a chair outside the shop.

"Marcantuono!... Good morning," he said offering his hand for a handshake. "Have you picked up the registered letter?"

There was nothing, absolutely nothing secret in that village; everybody knew everybody's affairs.

Marcantuono confided his difficulties and soon, Mr Collato produced an official form for the declaration. As a second witness they called the barber from his barber shop next door.

"Bad times," Marcantuono said sorrowfully, "when an honest man can no longer be trusted!"

Soon they were speeding for the post office to collect the letter.

It was a buff-coloured envelope, covered in stamps of many colours. He put it in his pocket while rushing home. His son wanted to read it immediately but his father cautioned him: "There are eyes and ears everywhere in this village, my son," he said, stretching his arm to put a finger on the boy's mouth.

Costanza laid the sauce on the stove and was about to start making fresh pasta. But not before she stationed her daughter at the doorstep to watch for her husband and son returning. Now and then she would shout: "Are they coining yet?"

"No, mama."

"For goodness sake! It takes them so long to pick up a letter."

It was nearly midday when the two appeared around the corner.

"Mama... Mama, they're coming!" Marietta shouted, all excited.

Costanza quickly wiped the flour off her hands and ran to the door. "Have you read it?... What does it say?... "

"We have not read it." Marcantuono replied showing the letter. They all sat around the table in the dining room.

"Open it and read it." said Marcantuono, speaking to his son.

Carminuccio opened it. Surprise, surprise! In the middle of two sheets of thick writing paper there was a cheque for two thousand dollars.

"Two thousand dollars?" Marcantuono could not believe it. "Why?" Why indeed... but two thousand dollars there were.

Costanza and the little girl sighed and stood still with open months. "Two thousand dollars!... and all you can do is call that cousin of yours a good-for-nothing!"

The boy started reading: "I do hope this letter finds you well... etc... etc... but, I am writing to you mainly to give you great news. You see, I have been proposed as a Senator... My proposers say... "

"My god... go on... go on," ordered Costanza.

"... they say my nomination would have a better chance of success if I could demonstrate noble ancestry in Italy, my country of origin. I have been told that we, the Marcantonios, are descended from the great Roman emperor Marcantonio.

"But our name is Marcantuono," interrupted the father.

"It is the same thing."

"Go on... "

"He says the two thousand dollars are for the costs of the search and says also that in recent times there was a prince called Marcantonio and that we are descended from that prince.

"He must be mad."

"What are you saying," admonished Costanza. "It may be true; what do you know?"

"Oh, papa... just think of it... us descended from princes!" Marietta was rapturous, but Marcantuono had no illusions: "I say this cousin of mine is not just a good-for-nothing, but also an idiot. We have always been farmers: my grandfather, my grandfather's grandfather. Always farmers."

"Yes, but gentlemen, noble farmers," intervened the girl who mixed well at school with the girls of good standing.

The boy, who had been observing all three of them, came up with the right solution.

"You never know," he said. "There is nothing to lose. We have got the money so why not ask advice from an acknowledged expert in these things?" The poor man let himself be convinced. He got up and started pacing the room with a scowling expression on his face: "Marcantuono:... the imperial farmer... Marcantuono the Emperor!... Ridiculous!"

"Papa... " Marietta interrupted. "Marcantonio... Marcantonio!"

He made a gesture of annoyance and went to the bedroom for a rest.

Next day Mr Marcantuono went to see his friend Mr Collato at the tobacco shop. Mr Collato had been a non-commissioned officer with the Finance Police and his advice was always appreciated by Marcantuono. He took the letter and firstly took a long look at the stamps, visibly marvelling, then took out the written message and read it right through without blinking an eye. Having finished reading, he took off his spectacles and burst into a rumbling laugh.

"He is mad!... Quite mad!" was his judgement, spacing the words at regular intervals between the laughs. Having noted Marcantuono unamused stare, he recomposed himself: "Are you serious?" he asked.

"Mmm... well ... if it can be of help to this good-for-nothing cousin of mine to become a Senator... "

Mr Collato was left thinking and looking very amused. He had another laugh, a discreet one this time, and looked straight into Marcantuono's eyes: "True... " he said. "True!" He looked as if he were wracking and searching his brain for an answer, when suddenly he became serious, adding: "A great honour for our village! The son of one of our people Senator of the United States; it would be great, what a great honour!" Marcantuono looked at him and instantly felt quite important, setting himself in a pose of wry satisfaction. "So, what shall I do?" he asked.

Mr Collato had another long silent search. Suddenly he thought he had found the answer: "That's it. I shall write a letter for you to Dr Cerino, a solicitor friend of mine in the provincial capital. He is a very smart fellow; he will certainly know where to start."

Being a man in the habit of hearing all sorts of strange and queer tales, Dr Cerino read the letter from Collato with a cunning, wry smile, and as usual in the profession, in order to cause a sort of nervous anxiety, did not reply until a week later.

> "Dear Mr Marcantonio,
> With reference to the letter from Mr Collato, a dear friend of mine, regarding your American cousin, I wish to tell you that I find the problem very interesting and that we have presently initiated the necessary searches.
> Yours faithfully,
Dr Cerino M.F.G.I.

Two weeks later, Mr Marcantuono was invited to go to the provincial capital, to the legal office of Dr Cerino.

The waiting room, with a large bookcase on one side and a tall open window on the other, was full of people sitting on an assortment of wooden chairs and old sofas. Father and son sat waiting to be called. Among a good number of persistently annoying flies there was a big bluebottle buzzing around the room quite close to the heads of those poor people, some of whom showed real affliction in their worried faces. A thoughtful little man was tapping his foot at regular intervals on the majolica pavement, sighing and yawning nervously, showing a mouth with hardly any teeth; a quite obese lady, with sharp eyes and a neck full of custom jewellery, was sweating profusely while she tried to swat the bluebottle with a handkerchief. Meanwhile the bluebottle, insistently attracted perhaps by some sort of perfume, looked determined to pierce her forehead with diabolical speed.

After nearly an hour, father and son were led to Dr Cerino's office. As soon as he saw them enter, the solicitor jumped up from the swivel chair behind the desk and went to meet them with the widest of smiles.

"Ah... Mr Marcantonio! How are you? Do come and sit down. Who is this? Your son? What a handsome boy! Please... please."

"My name is Marcantuono, sir."

"Ah. Not Marcontonio," he said, looking at some notes. "Of course, of course."

Dr Cerino pulled a large green file out of his desk and began humming, as though talking to himself.

"Hum... ah... yes... hum... very good." He rested the paper on the desk and stared right into Marcantuono's eyes. "It is very promising. My colleague has undertaken exhaustive research, which has established and confirmed that a Roman Emperor named Marcantonio reigned in the years 140–180 AD. His real name was, in fact Marcus Antoninius and, according to legend, he left numerous offspring, some of whom later became Emperors themselves. These offspring, I mean the sons, travelled and settled in every corner of the Empire; in Cappadocia, in Macedonia, in Gaul and in Italy. His search has reached the year 1700. As you can see, he has done a great deal of work and is presently preparing a report on the Marcantonio families up to 1850. For later years he will have to do more research.

"But, excuse me, Doctor, what has this Marcus got to do with it?"

"Papa, it is the same name in Latin."

"You have a very intelligent son, Mr Marcontonio."

"Marcantuono, Doctor... Marcantuono."

"Oh yes... oh yes... " said Dr Cerino when he regretfully realised that his tactic of instilling a measure of false pride and vanity into Marcantuono had failed.

"For the moment," continued Dr Cerino, "there is nothing more we can do, but I am sure we will succeed in untying every knot in the end, as it is commonly said. Meanwhile, you will understand that we have gone into a lot of expense: travel, hotels, gratuities, etc. so if you do not mind, we would appreciate something on account. But, of course, if you wish also to pay for the work my colleague is doing in preparing a further report, do as you see fit." He pushed a button under the desk and as quick as you can say boo, an elegant young woman came in full of smiles.

"My secretary will fix everything," said Dr Cerino getting up from his chair to lead the Marcantuonos to the door. He again put a hand on the boy's shoulder and quite affably said:

"What a handsome boy!... Well, goodbye."

The young lady led them to a room in the corridor. "Here we have the usual problem," she said. "Do you need a receipt or not?"

"It does not matter," answered Marcantuono.

"Well;" the young woman continued sweetly, "your bill comes to 980.000 lire."

Marcantuono took out his wallet and handed her the money. On the way out Carminuccio warned his father that they would have to show his American cousin how they spent the money, so they decided to go back and ask for a receipt.

The young lady was quite furious. "I asked you if you needed a receipt, did I not?"

"Yes," muttered Marcantuono. "But we must show to our cousin what we spent."

"This way we will lose money; we would have to pay taxes. My calculations were based on not issuing a receipt, which meant giving you a discount." She then lifted the telephone and spoke to Dr Cerino.

"They have come back," she said. "They now want a receipt." Dr Cerino had no time to waste; he cut short the conversation.

"Dr Cerino says you are good people; it is all right this time."

They took the receipt and went out for some shopping, but it was nearly one o'clock and most shops had already closed. They had to wait for re-opening time at four o'clock. After buying things which could not be obtained in the village, they were on their way to the van at the parking lot when, among a crowd of people out for their customary walk, they spotted Dr Cerino. Mr Marcantuono found himself face to face with him. He politely took off his hat but Dr Cerino, who was with an elegant lady hurried straight past him without the slightest acknowledgement.

"That was Dr Cerino," said the boy. "He did not answer your greeting."

"My dear son, they meet so many people. They have to remember who is and who is not a delinquent," he said so not to appear humiliated.

When they got home Costanza anxiously asked: "Well, what have you learned?"

"Nothing!.. Nothing, mama." replied the boy.

"That is not true," intervened Marcantuono. "We have learned that solicitors lose money."

*

"But my dear, dearest friend," remarked Mr Collato in a teasing tone, sitting on the doorstep of his son's shop, after hearing about Marcantuono's interview with Dr Cerino. "You have been done; led around by the nose. Nearly a million lire – Crazy... crazy!"

"He said they had incurred a lot of expenses," said Mr Marcantuono attempting to minimise his naiveté.

"How can you stop a friend being a solicitor? You tell me. On all accounts; what use are they these seventeenth-century people? It is a swindle, I tell you. I sent you to him to get advice, not to start a search, true or not. Listen to me," continued Mr Collato. "Save yourself more money... "

"It is not mine... "

"That is unfair to your cousin."

"You are right; sorry," said Marcantuono in a contrite tone.

Mr Collato went on: "Listen; you go to the local Registrar's Office and also to the provincial one, and ask them to fish out every ancestor of yours as far back as they can, without spending a penny."

"Do you think a prince will come out of it?"

"I give you a one percent probability, but at least you will not spend any money."

Marcantuono's wife, who was already looking forward to the thoughts of and feelings of nobility, encouraged her husband to follow this other piece of advice from Mr Collato.

"All right! What can we lose."

A few days later, father and son set out for the provincial capital... to no avail. Before they could even state their case, a civil servant made them wait more than ten minutes at the counters on account of a long argument with a young lady typist on the subject of operatic music. When he was told what the two were there for and especially when he was told what they were looking for, he burst into thunderous laughter. He went back to the young typist and, having muttered a few words in her ear, they both went into stitches.

"My dear fellow," said the civil servant after partially regaining his composure, "if you are looking for your near ancestors, there is the Communal Registrar. If you are looking for nobility, there is the Heraldic Office in Rome. If you care to wait a moment, I'll give you the address." and went back to mock and laugh with the young girl. After a long pause, he came back to the counter with a mischievous smile on his face and, before handing over the piece of paper with the address, he asked: "Are you peasants?"

Marcantuono was dumbfounded.

"Do me a favour, go to hoe."

Marcantuono became white with anger but he was unable to utter any words. He took the address and like a scolded dog, led his son into the street and there he began to give vent to his anger.

"Enough, enough!" he kept shouting between the usual swear words. "He is right, you know, it is the end; to hell with nobility."

Twelve days later the report came from Dr Cerino; three long typewritten pages. He was about to throw it away into the fire but, on second thoughts, he ordered his son to read it. "We have paid for it, anyway."

The first two pages told of the enquirer's journeys: the hotels, the towns; the third was all about the discoveries and the progress made.

In Genoa in the year 1721, a Marcantonio, who was said to belong to a noble family, was hanged for piracy on the high seas.

... in Venice, around 1737, a certain Marcanto, which is the same as Marcantonio in dialect, a rich merchant in silk and spices, was sent to a penal colony in Dalmatia, for fraud and burglary.

... in Naples, a certain Marcantoniello, killed his wife and ran away to the Americas.

... in Rome there had been a Bishop and a Cardinal both named Marcantonio but it had been impossible to find their origins."

The narrative concluded: "To continue our search after the seventeenth century, more funding will have to be provided. In this respect, please contact my secretary."

"I will show this letter to Mr Collato, we will have a great laugh: do we have to pay to be informed of the kind of people we are descended from? I think we should write to that good-for-nothing cousin of mine and tell him what we have discovered. Take pen and paper and write what I tell you."

Carminuccio collected the necessary items and started writing as his father dictated.

"Dear Cousin Marcantuono... Put a line under uono. To tell you the truth, we are ashamed of what we have discovered: a corsair, a robber, a murderer and some Cardinals. I am afraid there is no nobility in our family... no Dukes and no Princes... "

"But father," interrupted little Marietta, "at school the other day the teacher was talking about Cardinals; she said they are Princes, Princes of the Church!"

The Final Instalment

To put it mildly, the word "stupid" was beginning seriously to get on his nerves. It was the term by which his master, rightly or wrongly, chose to address him every time there was reason to reproach him. However, it was a term that Pasqualino had often heard, almost as though it was his real name, but it still sounded abusive in his ears. Therefore, when Don Giacinto hurled it at him for the umpteenth time to indicate how senseless his proposal seemed to be, it sent a shiver of anger coursing through his blood. He had no doubt; someday his resentment would boil over and he would finally challenge the master, a man he respected more than anyone else in the world. He would tell him bluntly that he no longer wanted to hear that word uttered. It was not nice, especially when spoken in front of other people. For the time being, though, he resisted the temptation and swallowed his pride. But he stood firmly by his resolution: he no longer wanted to be a shepherd. He wanted to be transferred to the stables and become a mule-rider.

"Oh, come on, do not be so stupid," Don Giacinto said casually. "Who, then, is going to look after the sheep?"

"Let young Ronzino do it. He is a good boy," replied the shepherd.

"Ronzino? Do not be so stupid," Don Giacinto said again, bristling his shoulders in a gesture of annoyance. He was about to turn on his heel and walk away when Pasqualino resolutely stepped in front of him in a manner that surprised them both.

"I am serious Don Giacinto, I do not want to be a shepherd any more."

Don Giacinto became slightly agitated by this temerity.

"What is it now," he shouted, adopting a slightly defensive posture, for he had seen on the boy's face a look of resolution that had been quite unthinkable before.

Pasqualino turned to pleading: "Please master, give me the job with the mules; I must have the job with the mules."

His attitude and the tone of voice he had used when stepping in front of Don Giacinto could not be mistaken: it was a challenge. In the boy's eyes Don Giacinto spotted rebellion. For a moment he had felt quite intimidated, but the pleading in Pasqualino's voice softened his attitude.

This was a completely new situation: was he further to consider the lad in front of him still as a boy, as someone who, rather than be told what to do, had the temerity to stand up and ask for what he wanted? Or should he readjust his thinking to the new situation and agree to the boy's request? Was it true? Had this boy really become a man? He found this hard to believe, so he persisted in his usual tone: "Have you lost your senses? Are you stupid?"

"Not at all," replied the boy in a firm voice, "I just must have the job with the mules."

Don Giacinto paused for a while, then, in a softer tone of voice he asked again: "What about the sheep?"

"Ronzino is very clever with the sheep. He is a big boy now, nearly twelve and he is also very brave."

Don Giacinto was thinking hard. The boy had a well-developed, muscular physique that was ideal for loading and unloading the mules. Perhaps, after all, it was a good idea but he did not want to lose face by giving way too quickly. So he said:

"Working with the mules is very difficult, you know. It is not at all like lazing around in the fields all day with the sheep."

"I know," replied the boy.

"Well, I have always thought you were silly, but you can have your way. Go to the stables and start right away." Don Giacinto turned his back on Pasqualino and went off towards the farm snorting and fuming.

So Pasqualino took charge of a pair of mules used to transport wheat and other cereals to the wholesaler in the village, an hour's walk away along a dirty track. He had been a good shepherd, but even before he had resolved on this inauspicious plan, he thought it would be a good idea to work with the mules, going up and down to the village. He was bound to meet many people and he was sure that he would feel at home among them.

He was a shy boy, normally introverted and he had been conditioned by the solitude of the grazing fields, day after day, in all sorts of weather. He had been pondering a plan for which he needed the mules. He was nineteen and had spent almost all his life on the farm, that is since his parents, who had themselves been in service all their lives to Don Giacinto's family, had suddenly died leaving him an orphan at the age of seven. His father had been the best cheese-maker in the district and his mother had been a housemaid to Donna Luigina.

It was already harvest time; the July sun beat down mercilessly on the sheaves and the soil was hot and dry. On the threshing compound other mules walked around in circles endlessly crushing the sheaves to dust. In another compound, two men were winnowing with wooden forks to separate the grains from the straw.

Almost unnoticed, Pasqualino entered the compound and quickly began to load the mules, lifting the sacks without any help from the men working nearby, and left for the village.

On the cobbled street that led to the village square the gossip-mongers, young girls working at their embroidery frames and old women darning socks while sitting in the cool shade outside their front doors, continued making spiteful remarks about the identity of the young man and his animal-like physique. Now and then, their remarks were tinged with humour and malice.

"Who is he...? Who is he not...? Someone from another village...?"

Finally a little old lady dared to ask: "Here, boy, who are you?"

Pasqualino went as red as a beetroot: "I am Pasqualino, from Don Giacinto's farm," he said, continuing on his way with his eyes downcast and staring at the cobblestones.

The curiosity that had been quite contained in their mistrustful glances for a considerable period, was daily becoming more and more pitiful if not morbid.

"What is happening to him?" they asked themselves, giggling.

In fact as the days passed the boy's appearance became more and more shabby. His clothes looked increasingly the worse for wear, while his face and knees were continually covered in fresh scratches that could be seen through the holes and tears in his trousers.

"Is his master beating him?"

"No, surely not!"

"What's happening to him, then?"

All the girls hid behind the shutters on their windows and laughed shamelessly as he passed by. But Pasqualino went on his way unconcerned, fixing his obstinate stare on the cobbles which rang to the sound of steel-clad hooves.

By now, everyone knew that he was the son of the old cheese-maker and Maria Pituzza, who had been in service with Don Giacinto.

"Don Giacinto beating him? It is not possible. He is quite haughty and occasionally quick-tempered, but not violent. Anyway, somebody beating a boy with a physique like his?" It was a real mystery.

Don Giacinto had noticed the slow and shameful transformation with disgust. Several times he had reproached Pasqualino sternly, adding that hateful word:

"What is it?.. What is happening to you, will you tell me? I cannot imagine that anyone is beating you; you are not so stupid as to let anyone do that."

Beside himself with anger, he finally took Pasqualino aside one day and told him that unless he explained why he had let himself go in such a shameful way, he would have no alternative but to beat it out of him. "...And then we'll see whether you have the courage to lift a hand against me or not. After all, I have been like a father to you these many years. I am disgusted and ashamed. Just look at the way all the local people are staring at you and laughing at you in the threshing compound."

"It is none of their business," Pasqualino said throwing a challenging glance at the compound, where some of the workers suddenly seemed preoccupied with their work.

"It is my business, though," shouted Don Giacinto. "Just look at what is happening to the mule. Do you think I have not noticed that it is limping and covered in scratches and cuts? You must have gone crazy, there is no other explanation."

Pasqualino lowered his head in shame and did not reply. He was a man in mental torment and, struggling with his regret, he looked a very sad sight indeed. Twice, Don Giacinto raised his hand as though to hit him, but he was able to control himself and finally noticed the looks of amusement on the faces of the few farm hands who had witnessed the scene. He lost his patience and decided to make an example of Pasqualino that would restore his authority. Once more he tried to get an answer to his questions, but Pasqualino would not be intimidated.

"That's it, then!" he shouted. "You are fired. Take your belongings and go. Get out of my sight!" As he said this, he turned on his heel and glared at the other men. "And you lot can all get back to work too, or you'll all be next for the sack!" With that, he strode off towards the farm buildings.

Pasqualino was left dumbfounded. His heart was thundering in his chest and a shiver ran through his body. Like diamonds glinting in the last rays of the setting sun, two tears sprang from his eyes and ran down his cheeks, creating wet streaks on his muddy and scratched face.

The farm hands giggled to themselves and went back to work and everything returned to normal: the sheep calmly continued grazing and the sun sank into the forest, painting the clouds a blazing red and flashing beams of light through the oak branches. The crickets had also begun their nightly song earlier than usual.

As he had been told to do, Pasqualino left the mules there and then and, once he had collected some of his belongings from his room above the stables, he strode off towards the mountain and the forest, taking a further step closer to his destiny.

Dusk was falling and the full moon was just visible now, hanging like a huge silver disk in the immensity of space. It shone through the fleeting clouds, caressing the broken branches in the clearing that were the witnesses to an effort that, one way or the other, was not going to be defeated. Pasqualino was undergoing training that allowed for no uncertainties and he felt that victory was bound to be his in the end.

Don Giacinto, he thought, had been right to dismiss him, but none of that mattered now. He felt both regret and shame, but how was he to justify an act that stemmed from desperation without having to reveal the object of the action?

The shrill song of the crickets echoed through the soft and caressing rustle of the leaves on the trees above his head while he tried desperately to sleep. He tossed and turned in torment on his straw pallet under the stars until finally, exhausted, he fell into a fitful sleep. As he slept he was troubled by vivid and disturbing dreams.

At daybreak, he awoke to the sound of a flute in the distance. He walked to the edge of the forest and spotted Ronzino, sitting on an old tree trunk playing the flute while guarding the sheep. It was a beautiful morning, the air was clean and crisp and there was a touch of dew on the lower leaves and the grass. It was the kind of day that would have put a smile on his face had his situation not been so desperately sad and depressing.

He returned to his hiding place in the forest. The new suit which, some days previously, he had picked up from the tailor in the village, was hanging from a low branch on the tree trunk and was moving to and fro in a sort of ghostly dance. He had made great sacrifices for that suit and he still had not paid the final instalment.

He sat on the straw sack staring into the emptiness of the place, and began to reminisce and ponder on his life. The pleasant parts of it made him emotional.

He saw himself as a boy of seven when, having lost his parents of whom he had no clear recollection, he remained at the farm and was treated like a son, as Donna Luigina used to say to him. In no time, however, he had to earn his keep and was put to look after the sheep and help the shepherd who emigrated to South America a few years later. From then on he never left the farm where he dealt with all sorts of chores: from cleaning the stables to providing water for the household and the stables. He cleaned Don Giacinto's boots, the saddles, implements and did many other chores until, exhausted, he would slump on his mattress in the stables and sleep peacefully until morning. Then there was Raffaella, who did nothing but torment him with her impossible games.

Some two years younger than Pasqualino, she was Don Giacinto's only daughter and she used to try his patience to the limit in between his chores. However, he would never rebel. She was badly spoiled and quite a chatterbox. She had no one else to play with, so she took merciless advantage of Pasqualino's quiet character and submissive nature. Dreaming, perhaps, of becoming an Amazon, she would make him go down on his knees like a horse, sit on his back and drive him using a cane as a whip on his backside. Sometimes his knees bled, then he would excuse himself and laugh it off as though it were only a joke. Sometime later Martello came along!

Why she had to call the horse Martello, which means hammer in Italian, was beyond his understanding. Perhaps it was because he had such a flat nose and nodded his head up and down, as if he was hammering in a nail. The little horse replaced him in the attentions of the "Signorina", who was now fifteen years old and beginning to show signs of a flourishing beauty. On top of all his other chores he had to look after Martello: "Woe betide you if you neglect him," she would warn. So Pasqualino kept him clean, fed and watered him, changed his pallet every day and saddled him when she wanted to ride him, her tiny foot in his hand, she would spring into the saddle like a gazelle and gallop off leaving a scent of violets and freesias in her wake.

She left to study at college in the provincial capital, but would return to the farm every weekend to ride Martello. Sometimes she brought a number of showy idlers back with her, boys and girls who made a lot of noise. From where he stood on the grazing ground, he could hear the garrulous giggles of the girls. On these occasions he preferred to be far away, for they used to look at him with cold indifference. However, he was often called into the stables when she wanted to display her skills. So Pasqualino kept cleaning and saddling the horse, blushing red as a beetroot and trembling, while the scent of freesias and violets filled the air as she galloped off, leaving him to gaze after her enchanted.

All those good-for-nothing friends were there that day. Faintly, but still audible, the sound of laughter and giggling came to him. To him they were like the stings from a swarm of bees, and just as poisonous.

The sun was moving slowly towards its zenith, turning the air from pleasantly warm to hot and down on the farm all seemed to be calm.

Inside the house, however, it was a different story. Don Giacinto had become so fed up with the continuous scolding from Donna Luigina and Raffaella that he avoided as far as possible having anything to do with them in the house.

"What kind of madness possessed you?... Our poor Pasqualino! God only knows where he might be... and maybe without a bite to eat," Donna Luigina sulked. "You must be out of your mind!"

"My little horse; all dirty. Who is going to look after him now?" whined Raffaella.

"You will have to go and look for him, even if you have to beg forgiveness! We have no water, the stairs are dirty and we have no logs for the bread-oven. You must get him back... poor boy.

"Me?... go and look for him... ask his forgiveness? You must both be demented!" Don Giacinto shouted while making for the stairs without looking back.

After his bout of rage that had led to Pasqualino's dismissal, Don Giacinto had actually regretted his action. But to prostrate himself to that ungrateful boy who was, after all, only a servant was totally unthinkable.

"A servant. Yes, a servant rebelling against his master. After all the good we have done for him."

When Raffaella went down to the stables and found Martello dirtier than ever she went into a frenzy. She rushed to heir mother almost in tears. "What shall I do, what shall I do, mama?"

"That ungrateful boy should come back and ask Father's forgiveness, that's what he should do. Maybe we can get some men to go and look for him. Yes, he is ungrateful and inconsiderate."

"He was a good boy, the poor boy!" Donna Luigina kept whimpering.

"No, mama; somehow of late he seemed quite strange. It is almost as though he hated me."

"What are you saying, girl? You are mistaken, he loved us all... You are wrong."

But Donna Luigina had some misgivings herself. She, too, had noted some changes in Pasqualino. He had become even more uncommunicative. No longer would he stop to chat when he brought the fresh water to the house. In fact, as soon as he had deposited the barrels on the wooden stand, he looked as though he was standing on hot coals and anxious to run off. "Good day," was all he used to say.

Donna Luigina loved that boy. Almost always alone in those big rooms full of stagnant shadows, she welcomed his company. It was from him that she learned about this and that, because she was never able to extract more than a few words from her husband. Don Giacinto would do and undo things in his own way and would not be contradicted.

"Poor boy... poor boy," she would say to everyone she met, and to herself she insisted: "Hate my little girl? Impossible!"

Several days passed and, to everyone's consternation, Pasqualino did not reappear. The threshing was finished and on the threshing floor, a large amount of straw basked in the hot sun. With the rapid approach of the festival of their patron saint, all the farm hands had left for the village and so had the "Signorina's" friends, while she herself was in a perpetual state of moodiness.

The mules, along with the sheep were grazing in the meadow. Only Martello, in the stable, was left to suffer the indignity of a filthy pallet.

*

There were only two days to go to the start of the festivities.

One night late, after taking a circuitous route along country paths and narrow village streets, so as to avoid meeting anybody, Pasqualino stealthily reached the centre of the village. At that hour of the night – almost eleven, everyone was asleep after a long day of hard work and a meagre dinner. In small villages, where there is nothing else to do except work and sleep, people go to bead early. The streets were deserted and the few electric lights, instead of lighting the street, contributed to creating fearful patches of mysterious shadows. Now and then a cat would jump out of the darkness, ruffled by disturbance and, after a long stare at the intruder, with its yellow flashing eyes, it would hiss loudly then bolt, either behind a wall or through a hole in a door. As on every other hot night, the crickets continued screeching and asserting a realm of permanent monotony. Here and there a solitary firefly flashed her semaphore messages into the night, but what really stressed of the dreariness of the night was the barking of dogs, who seemed to be calling to each other from the various streets in the village.

Pasqualino had no fear of dogs, in fact he had once stood up to a wolf, chasing it away with stones. He continued on his way and cautiously reached one of the doors in a narrow alley. He knocked loudly on the door.

In villages in this part of Italy there is nothing more dreaded than a knock at the door late at night. Don Ciccio awoke with a start.

"Good heavens," his wife cried in terror. "What can it be... my poor mother, some accident perhaps."

"Keep calm, just keep calm," Don Ciccio said reassuringly while slipping on his trousers. "OK, OK, I'm coming, just wait a bit, will you?" he shouted in reply to the insistent knocking. He went through the front room where he kept his sewing machine and where the main fireplace was with a large black pot hanging on a chain. "Who are you? What do you want?" he asked anxiously.

"I am Pasqualino, the shepherd."

"At this time of night? Good God in Heaven!"

"Who is it, who is it?" Don Ciccio's wife kept asking apprehensively.

"It's that..." He was about to utter the hated word "idiot", but managed to restrain himself. Instead he said: "It's that fellow I made the suit for. You know, the shepherd who works for Don Giacinto.

He opened the door to let him in, clearly showing how angry he was at being disturbed at such an ungodly hour.

"What do you want at this time of night?" Don Ciccio demanded.

"I want to pay the last Instalment on the suit you made for me," Pasqualino said.

"Holy Mary, could you not have waited until daylight at least?" Still grumbling, Don Ciccio let him in, while calling to his wife to go back to bed and that there was nothing to worry about.

Pasqualino paid the last ten lire due on the suit and, having collected his receipt marked "paid in full", he retraced his steps into the forest.

During the ten days of his absence in the depths of the forest he had eaten very little of substance; wild fruits, roots and the odd bird that he had been able to trap and roast over an open fire. As a result, he had lost a few pounds in weight. Less weight for the mule to carry, he thought wryly.

*

In the bright light of sunrise, the thunderous noise of fireworks coming from the distant village proclaimed the start of the Festival of St. Rock, the patron saint of the village. A thunderous noise that echoed through the valleys and the harvested fields, it was a call to merrymaking – the reward for a whole year of hard work, when even the poorest families celebrated by having meat for dinner and the children were allowed to gorge themselves on nuts and ice-cream.

At an early hour in the morning the brass band of Ferrandina was parading through the village, followed by a large bunch of children all dressed in their best attire bought by their parents' hard-earned savings. At the farm soon after the fireworks that started the festival, Don Giacinto and his family, those farm hands still in service and even Ronzino, the shepherd, were preparing to leave for the village. The sheep had been confined in the fold, the mules had been fed and watered, and on the threshing floors silence reigned. Having helped his wife and daughter into a gig cart and given them the reins controlling the old mare, Don Giacinto slipped his best shotgun into the leather cover attached to the saddle, saddled his horse and, placing himself at the head of the convoy, led them all down to the village.

Pasqualino observed the whole scene from behind a bush at the edge of the forest and later returned to his hiding place through the thick scrub to wait for the time for the games and competitions to start. A feverish anxiety tormented him; he could not remain still for a single instant. Was this really a passion or an obsession? Was it madness or just a desire to destroy himself because he felt his life was useless? He felt he was in a prison of loneliness, that he was inadequate and his hatred increased against everyone and everything. His desire was to vindicate himself by sacrificing himself in a gesture of contempt. Or was his passion just an excuse?

He began to reason with himself: Maybe it is just a useless sacrifice. But then a voice in his head argued: "How could you bear to live with just the perfume of freesias and violets and nothing else?"

"I'll kidnap her, that's what I'll do."

"Oh yes, brilliant plan! But what about your everlasting gratitude to her family, and then there is your debt of honour to redeem?"

"You are right. I must redeem my debt of honour."

The devil inside him would always win these discussions, and all because of that delicate perfume and the dainty foot she would use to leap lightly onto the back of her patient little horse.

Soon after midday the sky over the village became dotted with tiny white clouds, signalling that the procession of the saint was coming to an end with the customary fireworks. It was still very hot, but a light breeze had begun to stir the leaves on the higher branches of the trees. The fireworks eventually stopped. He then imagined all the villagers sitting down to dinner, to be followed by a siesta and the immobility of a hot afternoon when the crickets have the world to themselves. He was terribly restless.

That afternoon he heard the sound of a brass band faintly in the distance and saw himself again as a little boy, just like any other boy, following it through the streets of the village, spellbound.

Slowly, the villagers began to emerge from their houses after the siesta and began milling around in the square and the main street. The Church of St. Rocco had been left open all day and the Saint himself seemed to be a participant at the feast in his honour. Surrounded by hundreds of candles, he seemed to be quite pleased. The church itself had thick rustic walls which made the interior very cool, conveying a feeling of serenity and peace. The only decorations were an extraordinary complex of religious paintings covering the wall behind the altar in a dizzying array. People milled around lighting candles and looking at the other statues, enjoying the delicious coolness offered by those massive walls.

At about six o'clock Don Comodo, the priest, arrived at the church to conduct the Vespers service. He was accompanied by the sacristan and a number of lower clerics. When everyone was in the church he said mass, finishing by thanking God for a bountiful harvest. Afterwards, the clearing, the road near the church, the balconies and windows filled with people from the village and the surrounding area, all of whom had come to join in the games or run in the St. Rock Palio race.

The race, or Palio, was a sort of manual dexterity race run under a rope strung between two poles. From the rope hung a large cork to which a brass ring had been inserted into it. The riders, on horses and mules, competed to thread a long pointed stick into the ring – a task made doubly difficult when the wind contrived to make things worse.

Pasqualino had been training hard for this event, and felt that he had ten times the chance of winning the ring than anyone else. Of course, no one suspected this.

The course, between two thick lines of spectators, was ready and, one by one, the competitors arrived to rapturous applause. First, they stopped at the judge's bench to pay their entry fee then they proceeded to the starting line. The crowd were talking about the chances each of the runners had, anxiously awaiting the start when, from the northern side of the course, Pasqualino appeared riding his faithful mule who was still limping slightly. Trotting merrily, and amid whistles and catcalls from the crowd, he went to the organiser's bench to pay his entry fee. They had to consult with each other on whether late entries were allowed, but finally they agreed and he took his place among the other competitors.

Don Giacinto and all his family, including brothers, sisters, nephews and nieces were among the spectators at the horse race. They were all staying at his aunt's house which had a long balcony that made an ideal grandstand from which to watch the proceedings. When they spotted the boy on the limping mule they could not believe their eyes. Donna Luigina felt quite relieved and Raffaella applauded and laughed gaily.

The competitors began the first run, galloping along the main road, almost coming to a stop under the rope, but all to no avail. Pasqualino missed twice himself. He had been clumsy at the beginning, because he had spotted Raffaella on the balcony. Indeed it looked as though all his efforts and sacrifices, the petty humiliations, hunger and pain, including the barbs of Don Giacinto's rage were going to be in vain. Without that ring there would be nothing left for him in life but despair and oblivion. He had to win that ring, cost what it may. He gathered himself for a final effort and, as he came within a few yards of the rope, he produced a small stick he had concealed on his saddle, aimed at the ring and caught it on the end of the stick. The mule trotted quietly the whole time and did not even have to stop. The crowd who had earlier jeered at him, now burst into wild and excited applause.

"He has taken it… he has taken it!"

"Who has?"

"The fellow in the corduroy suit."

"Yes, but who is he?"

"His name is Pasqualino. He is the shepherd who works for Don Giacinto."

The crowd were still applauding as Pasqualino approached the organisers' bench to exchange the brass ring for a gold one with a small diamond set in it. The ring itself nestled in a straw-coloured velvet box.

Don Giacinto could not believe his eyes. Smiling wryly he could not help but applaud just like everyone else on the balcony. In retrospect, he seemed to understand the reason why Pasqualino had been so secretive, and why there had been the small wounds on the boy and the mule.

"You know," he whispered to Dr Pietrone, "I would never have believed it. He has been training for this for weeks."

"Well done," agreed Dr Pietrone. "One of your own men, you must feel very proud. Bravo, bravo."

"I had nothing to do with it. In fact, I recently gave him the sack."

"Really?" Dr Pietrone said. "What a pity," and then added: "Poor boy."

Donna Beatrice, the old lady who owned the house, was passing around the lemonade when the last applause faded as Pasqualino rode away. She was a very perceptive woman and was, perhaps, the only one to perceive Pasqualino's feelings for her niece. The whole affair made her feel quite uneasy. She only hoped that it would all fizzle out, but seeing him under these circumstances made her very nervous.

Pasqualino left the happy crowd as though in a trance. In the other parts of the village there was hardly a soul. He made his way to the back of Donna Beatrice's house, looped the reins around a banister and moved towards the main door. It was a narrow street, the applause from the crowd and the sound of brass bands seemed to come from a million miles away.

He climbed the few steps to the front door and knocked. He was trembling like a leaf blown in the wind.

It was Donna Beatrice herself who came to open the door to him. When she saw him standing there stiff and tongue-tied, and hardly able to utter a word, she almost instinctively slammed the door in his face. Her age-worn face contorted in anger and she growled at him: "Well, what do you want?"

"Er, well, I'd like..." But he was unable to continue, so intimidating was the old lady's presence. Realising his predicament, he almost angrily thrust the box into the old woman's gnarled hand and said defiantly: "This ring is for Raffaella! Oh, and tell her that I love her," he flung over his shoulder as he jumped onto the mule's back and galloped off with all speed.

Donna Beatrice was left speechless. With the box in her hand and unable to move, she watched him recede into the distance as though in a dream. Had she been able to, she would have hurled the box from her.

When she regained control of herself, she spotted some of Raffaella's girlfriends nearby, laughing and smirking, and she realised they had heard every word of the exchange. Before she knew what they were doing, they had taken the box from her hand and had run off to tell Raffaella all about it laughing and joking.

"Oh, Raffaella, guess what just happened. The young man who just won the ring at the Palio was here. He said this ring is for you and he also said to tell you that he loves you. Isn't that nice, dear."

Poor old Beatrice was so dumbfounded that she hardly knew what she should do next. She dreaded the consequences of these revelations and felt bitter towards the girls because of their irresponsibility. For a few seconds she remained rooted to the spot. Then she tried to run after them and warn them to say nothing, but the physical effort was too great and she was overcome by a series of spasmodic convulsions. Guttural sounds, intended to be warnings, emanated from her throat. She was able to take a few steps in pursuit, but in the centre of the room she fell to her knees and collapsed in a dead faint.

Hearing the noise and commotion, and the sound of the old woman falling, everyone rushed in to see what had happened. Dr Pietrone went down on one knee beside the old woman and felt for a pulse.

"She's all right, she's not dead," he said. "It's only a fainting fit, thank God. Are there smelling salts in the house?"

Donna Luigina ran into the old woman's bedroom and emerged a few moments later carrying the smelling salts, which Dr Pietrone then held under the Donna Beatrice's nose.

When she came to, Donna Beatrice's first act was to look for the two girls, but they were circulating among the guests and showing off the ring, making jokes at Raffaella's expense. Soon, word of this reached Don Giacinto.

"What are you talking about? Have you gone mad or is this all true?" he exploded.

"Yes," answered one of the girls, "It is all true. This is what he said: 'This ring is for Raffaella and tell her that I love her.'"

She pushed the ring into Raffaella's hand and it felt as though a burning hot coal had been thrust upon her. Don Giacinto grabbed it from her hand and hurled it onto the floor. "The coward," he cried. Then, turning to his aunt he asked: "Is this true?"

The poor woman was unable to reply, but the look in her eyes spoke volumes.

Raffaella burst into tears and was consoled gently by her mother, Donna Luigina, who kept muttering that all this fuss and bother was for nothing. "There, you see? All this bother for nothing."

"For nothing, eh? I'll kill him, the ungrateful scoundrel!" Don Giacinto exploded. He seemed to have lost control of himself completely.

"Keep calm, please keep calm," Dr Pietrone admonished him kindly. "Otherwise you will he heading for a stroke. But Don Giacinto was becoming angrier by the minute. His rage knew no bounds.

"A stroke my foot!" exclaimed Don Giacinto. "He must have gone back to the farm to take the mule to the stables. If I find him there, I'll kill him," he said and grabbed his shotgun from behind the door. He ran to his horse that he had kept in a nearby stable and galloped off at full speed with his wife's entreaties ringing in his ears.

Very soon afterwards Dr Pietrone and Don Antonio, the pharmacist, followed him in the jig, lashing the horse to ever greater efforts. "We must stop him before he does something rash. He seems to have lost his mind completely."

Meanwhile, Raffaella had lapsed into a state of thoughtful calmness. Sitting in an easy chair in a corner, she let her mind drift into strange thoughts which were both frightening and euphoric at the same time. She remembered having felt him tremble every time she jumped into the saddle. Now she realised that it was not hate, but love that had motivated him.

Despite this realisation, she wanted him dead. "Yes, it is better this way," she said to herself. "One quick shot and it's all over!"

As soon as he arrived at the farm, Don Giacinto began searching everywhere: in the stables, the feed store, the piggery and the sheep-fold.

When the doctor and the pharmacist reached the farm they found Don Giacinto ranting and raving even louder than before: "You coward!... You ungrateful rascal! Where are you?"

Try as they might, the two friends were unable to make Don Giacinto see reason. He continued cursing and shouting, and rushing hither and thither. Suddenly, the sound of a braying mule came from the direction of the forest.

"The forest! That's where he is hiding," shouted Don Giacinto. "I'll have his hide before the day is out!" Off he rushed towards the forest, pursued by his two friends who were panting and out of breath.

When the three of them reached the clearing in which Pasqualino had made his base, they stopped dumbstruck. There, at the end of a rope he had tied to the branch of a tree, they found the lifeless body of Pasqualino.

The shock of the discovery sent cold shivers through every fibre of their beings. Don Giacinto let the shotgun fall from his nerveless fingers. Taking his courage in both hands, Dr Pietrone gingerly approached the tree. Close to the trunk was the boy's straw pallet, and hanging nearby was the new suit he had only worn once. Twice, he crossed himself. Just then he noticed a scrap of paper projecting from one of the boy's pockets. Maybe it was a message.

Carefully, so that he did not disturb anything, he extracted the paper and read it.

"What does it say?" asked the pharmacist.

"Nothing very interesting really. It just says: 'Pasqualino has paid the final instalment'."

Still wearing its harness, the mule went around quietly picking at blades of grass here and there. The crickets continued singing their summer melody while the setting sun, red as blood, filtered jets of light through the high branches of the trees.

"I swear to God, I would not have shot him." Don Giacinto kept mumbling in an emotional voice. "You must believe me; I swear to you."